praise for
History on a Personal Note

"Kirshenbaum has a strong moral aptitude and a ballistic sense of humor, launching anti-assumption rockets with cool precision.... Her candor about the female psyche is not unlike Margaret Atwood's, but her feisty voice, gutsy humor, mischievous dispassion, and gift for setting scenes and conjuring moments of realization are all her own." —*Booklist*

"Deceptively light in tone, these stories nevertheless carry weight, as do the characters.... A wide variety of styles and voices ... demonstrate Kirshenbaum's versatility and wit."
—*Publishers Weekly*

"Kirshenbaum uses her crisp prose and wry humor to illustrate home truths." —*Library Journal*

"Kirshenbaum practices the art of gossip as literature ... [she] is a fresh voice with a clear view of the causes and effects of what might be called boomer angst." —*Sun-Sentinel*

D0911049

STEPHAN BARKER

BINNIE KIRSHENBAUM is the author of five novels and two short story collections. She is a professor of fiction writing at Columbia University and lives with her husband in New York City.

history
on a personal
note

also by
Binnie Kirshenbaum

history
on a personal
note

stories

binnie
kirshenbaum

An Imprint of HarperCollinsPublishers

shed by Fromm International Publishing Corporation in
1995.

FIRST ECCO EDITION PUBLISHED 2004

Designed by Jeffrey Pennington

Library of Congress Cataloging-in-Publication Data

Kirshenbaum, Binnie.
    History on a personal note : stories / Binnie Kirshenbaum.—1st Ecco ed.
      p. cm.
    Contents: History on a personal note—For widgit stands—Money
honey—Faith is a girl's name—In the beginning—Carlotta—Halfway to
Farmville—White houses—Courtship—Jewish but not really—The zen of
driving—Viewing Stacy from above—Exclusive pleasures—A full life of a
different nature—The cape man—Rural delivery.
     ISBN 0-06-052089-2 (trade paper)
      1. United States—Social life and customs—20th century—Fiction.
2. Female friendship—Fiction. 3. Jewish families—Fiction. I. Title.

PS3561.I775H57 2004
813'.54—dc22

                 2003063127

04 05 06 07 08 BVG/RRD 10 9 8 7 6 5 4 3 2 1

In memory of my mot

acknowledgments

The story "Halfway to Farmville" was originally titled "Topsy Part 2" and was written and published in another form—two voices, one in poetry and the other in prose—as a collaboration with my best friend, the poet Susan Montez. Solely for the thematic purpose of this collection, I rewrote the piece. However, it is as much Susan's work as it is mine. And for it, among other things, I am grateful to her. I would also like to thank Dawn Raffel for the title.

For the story "Courtship," my parents were an inspiration.

The following stories were previously published: "Faith Is a Girl's Name" in *Asylum;* "In the Beginning" and "Jewish but Not Really" in *Word of Mouth II,* a Crossing Press anthology; "Carlotta" in *The Greensboro Review;* "Halfway to Farmville" was titled "Topsy Part 2" in *Sun Dog: The Southeast Review;* "White Houses" in *The Bridge;* "Viewing Stacy from Above" in *The Indiana Review;* "Money Honey" in *The New England Review/Bread Loaf Quarterly;* "A Full Life of a Different Nature" in *The Mid-American Review.*

contents

history
on a personal
note

A LEGENDARY YEAR: 1984
Whatever Happens, We Ought to See It Coming

Despite the theoretical knowledge that history repeats itself, Lorraine was devastated by a second Ronald Reagan landslide victory. In response, she declared herself a Communist, as if that would fix something or someone. This was Lorraine's take on Communism: Donald Trump would have to buy every woman in New York a gold and diamond tennis bracelet.

Me, I saw Reagan's second term as an inevitability. Not that the foresight made it any more palatable. It's just that I was prepared to be miserable.

Another thing Lorraine didn't see coming down the pike was her falling in love with Peter. Lorraine was a corporate travel agent, a career she chose for the benefits. Lorraine liked to fly in planes and stay in complimentary hotel rooms. Peter was one of her clients, a middleman who arranged jaunts for German tourists to places like Niagara Falls and Busch Gardens. Peter was also a German, and Lorraine referred to him as "that pain-in-the-butt Kraut who always wants discount rates and special favors." Often Lorraine responded to his requests by saying, "Hey, remember who won the war." Yet, one day she called me up and said, "Would you believe I've fallen in love with that pain-in-the-butt Kraut?"

Lorraine and Peter went mad for each other, but as Goethe once said, "The Germans are trouble to themselves and everybody else." This romance came with predicaments. Peter's stint in New York was temporary. He could, at any time, be transferred to some other country. He prayed it would not be Romania, where he was last, or anywhere in Africa because he had a fear of snakes. Another stone to trip them up along the path to bliss was the cross-eyed girl in the fox fur coat. Although he was not legally married to her, she and Peter had been living together for the past seventeen years. Their families were old friends residing in the same German gingerbread village, and that cheap-o tour company Peter worked for shipped them off to foreign lands, as if they were married, together.

Lorraine, hailing from south of the Mason-Dixon Line, would think about such things tomorrow. For now, she was in love, and she told me—although she never used such a word—that she and Peter were soul mates. "Southerners and Germans are one and the same," she said. "Both set out to enslave other peoples. We lost the wars we started. As a group, we're stupid as shit. And no matter where we go to, we have a strong attachment to our own soil, our land."

I, a Jewess, didn't know from such things. My people jumped like fleas from one place to another, never allowed to stay put long enough to form an attachment to the neighborhood. Even later, when history was kinder to my families, offering us haven in America, we moved a lot, upwardly mobile, until we wound up in a brand-new house, built just for us, in a suburb freshly developed. Raised up in one clip, it wasn't the sort of house that harbored ghosts. It had no past, no roots. Rather, one day we were there, and the next day we could be gone without a trace. My house could've been in the town that Hitler built for the Jews.

Lorraine tried to bake a *Flammkuchen* but didn't have the knack, and Peter couldn't develop a taste for peanut butter pie. But still, love flourished because, Lorraine explained, "The cross-eyed girl flatly refuses to give him a start-to-finish blow job. She won't swallow. Why do you think that is?" Lorraine asked me.

How could I possibly understand a people who consider swallowing a gob of jizz to be filthy, but found it conscionably clean to wash up with soap made from Jews, Gypsies, and priests? I shrugged, and Lorraine guessed, "It's one of those German peculiarities, isn't it?"

WILLKOMMEN: 1985–86
Reagan Honored SS Dead at Bitburg/
Peter Transferred Back to Frankfurt

Lorraine and Peter wrote long letters to each other. Lorraine lamented that his English was slipping fast. "*Sniks*, he writes," she told me. "He wrote that at least there are not *sniks* in Frankfurt. He meant *snakes*."

At work, Lorraine spent most of her days trying to finagle free airfare to Frankfurt. In December of 1986 she scored a pair of tickets from Lufthansa, and so I went with her to Germany.

While Peter and Lorraine made up for lost time in our freebie room at the Intercontinental Hotel, I went sightseeing. I did not go to museums and cathedrals. Rather, I went sight-seeing for Nazis. I sat around cafés clocking anyone old enough to have been one and tried to guess in which bit of nastiness they partook. Later, after Peter returned home to the cross-eyed girl, Lorraine and I went out for dinner. "Like that one there," I said, pointing to a table across from ours, indicating an old woman wearing one of those queer Tyrolean hats. "She either worked at a camp sorting clothes, pocketing whatever she could, or else she indoctrinated children, gathering them around her to read them that version of 'Hansel and Gretel' where the Jew tries to bake the little German children into matzo."

Lorraine nodded and remarked, "And where is the justice in this world that she sits here now eating that sausage like nothing ever happened?"

THE FOLLOWING DAY: 1986
Giving You a Number and Taking Away Your Name

Even after getting trapped on the Geisenerring, driving around and around it as if it were a maypole, as if there were no exit, and then having to stop for gas at the last-chance-for-gas station where the attendant stank from stale beer and looked like a serial killer, we managed to reach the border before nightfall.

Well-versed as to the ins and outs of travel restrictions, Lorraine outlined the plan for me. "We're allowed to go to West Berlin," she said. "So that's what we say. When they ask where we're going, we say Berlin. West Berlin."

Berlin was a good eight-hour drive from the border. We hadn't any luggage or enough money with us to make the trip. Also, Lorraine had a date with Peter for ten the next morning. Nonetheless, at each of the three checkpoints we handed over our passports and said, "West Berlin, *ja?*"

The guard in the third box directed us to the autobahn's far right lane. "You must stay on zis road. Zis is the road to Vest Berlin. Do not get off zis road."

Lorraine and I exchanged a glance. Then, she peered into the rearview mirror and hung a quick left. I played with the radio and picked up Radio Free Europe, or else it was the Armed Services Station. Whichever, we snuck into East Germany bopping to "Secret Agent Man," who gave you a number and took away your name. "Secret Agent Man," we sang along.

At a town called Eisenach, we stopped at a tacky roadside

winter carnival featuring a hand-cranked Ferris wheel. With a West German mark we bought two caramel-coated apples, which proved to be wormy, forcing us to go elsewhere in search of food.

The restaurant we found was a rustic place, stag heads mounted on stone walls. "I'll bet this used to be a scout camp for Hitler Youth," I said.

"That," Lorraine concurred, "or a hunting lodge for the SS."

We ordered the goulash, which wasn't half bad. Also having goulash were two Polish guys on holiday who kept popping up from their chairs to light our cigarettes. After dinner we found them, the two Polish guys, standing, under a light snowfall, beside our Opel Kadett, which was the only car in sight. They wanted a ride to somewhere, anywhere, but Lorraine said, "No. It's one thing if we get caught here. It'd be another story altogether if we get caught here with two Poles hiding in the backseat."

Our next stop was Weimar, the seat of a former German government, and a cute place in its own right, albeit somewhat tattered, the way an old silk love seat will fray at the edges. We walked the cobblestone streets to Goethe's house, but it was locked up for the night. Standing outside the door, Lorraine said, "He sure knew his people. Nothing but trouble is right."

The roads out of Weimar were lined with pine trees and very dark. There were no streetlamps, and a creepiness hung low like fog. "I feel like we're someplace hainted," Lorraine said. *Hainted*. That's how Southerners say *haunted*.

I got the map from the glove compartment and spread it open. "We're at Buchenwald," I told her.

Lorraine asked if I wanted to visit the camp, to take a tour. "I mean, as long as we're here. We could hop the fence."

It was very late at night, and that we were trespassing *behind* the Iron Curtain not withstanding, who breaks *into* Buchenwald? "Besides," I said, "if you want to keep your date with Peter, we'd better head back now."

"If we can get out of here, that is." Lorraine mentioned we might not be able to exit quite as easily as we'd entered. "You do realize we don't have the Berlin stamp on our passports."

I might've worried about that, except "Snoopy and the Red Baron" came on the radio, thus reducing any real concerns to a cartoon dogfight between a beagle and Von Richthofen, from which the beagle emerges victorious.

At the first checkpoint, we handed over our passports and got them back perfunctorily, like change at a tollbooth. "One down," Lorraine said.

The second guard flipped through the passports, then went back and turned the pages slowly. We watched him pick up a telephone, a hot line, and Lorraine suggested, "We might want to freshen our makeup. I think we're about to be interviewed. We ought to look our best."

Taking our compacts from our purses, crowding under the overhead car light, we applied lipstick and wiped mascara smudges from beneath our eyes. But, perhaps, for naught. Our passports were returned to us. The guard motioned for us to move on to the third checkpoint where four uniformed guards stepped out and surrounded our Opel Kadett. Lorraine turned to me and said, "This isn't good."

We were taken to an office that was bare except for one desk and three chairs. Lorraine and I sat as if we were there for a social visit. Pinned to one wall was a calendar with a picture of a German landscape, the sort that implies that this nation was never anything but fairy-tale cute.

The only guard who spoke English, and therefore the one who interrogated us, was young. All of eighteen. A chubby-cheeked baby. Thrilled with the responsibility of such an assignment, he demanded, "Vere did you go? Vith whom did you speak?" He aimed to be tough, but the flush in his face gave him away. "Vere did you go?" he asked again and again.

Again and again we told him we went only to Goethe's house, and that we didn't talk to anyone. "Weimar is a darling place," Lorraine said. "Just precious."

Sometime shortly before dawn, the Nazi/Communists concluded that we were nothing more than a pair of *Dummkopf* American girls who took a wrong turn. We were escorted to the border, and the four guards waved good-bye. "Weren't they sweet?" Lorraine said. "You know, considering."

We got back to the Intercontinental Hotel with just enough time for Lorraine to take a quick shower before meeting Peter in the lobby. I joined them as Lorraine was putting the finishing touches on the tale of our border crossing.

"But, Lorraine, ze four powers have agreed you must stay on ze Berlin autobahn." Peter was grinning, so tickled with her, his mistress, who'd gotten over on the system. Peter loathed not the East Germans, but their government and all Communists, whom he blamed for dividing his homeland.

FROM POLITICAL TO PERSONAL:
NOVEMBER 9, 1989
Like Jericho, the Walls Came Tumbling Down

I watched it on television, the destruction of the Berlin Wall and all it represented. Unlike the TV commentators, there was no joy in my heart. Unlike the line quoted ad nauseam—*Ich bin ein Berliner*—I was *not* one of them, and I liked that wall just as it was. To me, the wall spoke volumes. It said, "You get what you deserve."

When Lorraine and I were in Frankfurt, I found the West German affluence disturbing. I was bothered by the fox fur coats, by the number of Mercedeses on the road, by the ropes of sausages hanging in butcher shop windows, by the smell of fresh strudel wafting from bakeries. That they lived prosperously, that there was no daily rub to remind them of their fiasco in recent history, made it seem as if Germany were Monaco.

In the East, the comparative desolation was apt. It was fitting retribution for ex-Nazis to live behind barbed wire in a country where lighting was at a premium.

On a more personal note, although it wasn't Checkpoint Charlie, but some other checkpoint we'd crossed those three years ago, sneaking across an East/West border was now something we could never do again. An era was over.

Due to a series of mishaps spanning the globe, the cross-eyed girl learned that Peter was not skiing in Austria with his cousin Werner, but *fickening* with Lorraine in a hotel room overlooking Lake Como. A family conference was called, and all sides insisted Peter be a good German, an honorable German.

"I cannot zee you again," Peter told Lorraine, and he broke her heart for keeps.

Shutting off the television, I called Lorraine and asked, "Are you watching this?"

"I'm sick over it," she said. "Just sick. How in the world am I supposed to be a good Communist when the Communists can't be good Communists? Peter's probably so happy. He dreamt of this day. He hated that wall." Then, a thought occurred to her. "Maybe he'll see this as symbolic, inspirational, this tearing down of walls. Maybe he'll see the joy in breaking the rules, smashing the conventions." Lorraine was hoping this bit of anarchy would extend from the political to the personal.

I went back to the television and watched Germans dancing in their streets.

REUNIFICATION: OCTOBER 3, 1990
For Every Action There Is an Equal and Opposite Reaction

"A great day for freedom"—the anchorman on TV hailed the reunification of the two Germanys as reason to ring liberty bells. He obviously hadn't bothered to remember that twice before the Germanys united, Aryan forces joined Aryan forces and look what happened: world wars, mayhem, destruction, Buchenwald. Already, the Germans were looking toward Poland and licking their chops.

I combed the newspapers, letters to the editor, in search of another voice of protest, someone else saying, "Hey, wake up. Smell the coffee. A united Germany might not be such a bouquet of roses. We're talking here about a social climate where following orders is the equivalent of a life dedicated to prayer. Free elections don't necessarily yield Jeffersonian democracy. The last time a united Germany went to the polls, they voted the National Socialist ticket, remember?"

Although Lorraine and I could now drive to Weimar free as birds, who would want to? How sad would it be to blithely cross what was once a formidable border when "Secret Agent Man" would be just another golden oldie like "England Swings." No, Lorraine and I would never again revisit Goethe's house because of a triad of reunifications.

When Peter went and married the cross-eyed girl with the fox fur coat, Lorraine—like Lee at Appomattox—officially gave up. "My people aim to surrender with dignity," she said, "but surrender is always pathetic. We're a pathetic lot. If Jews were Southerners, you'd all be Holy Rollers by now."

Quietly, too quietly, Lorraine said she understood why Peter married his fellow German. "They share a common language," she said. "A culture, a collective guilt," and with that on her mind, Lorraine reunited with her homeland. She went south to a town called Dillwyn and married a gun-toting, cap-wearing, good ol' boy. They moved into a trailer and kept chickens in the yard. When Lorraine was seven months pregnant, they got a cow.

I couldn't have foreseen any of it. Yet, with the benefit of hindsight I was able to say, "There were signs."

1991: EVERYTHING CHANGES
Everything Stays the Same

All summer long the French were complaining about the Germans. The East Germans, the poor relations, the ones without a franc to spend, taking bus tours, day trips through Paris, jamming up the place without contributing to the local economy.

I read in the *Times* about the German real-estate developer who bought a plot of land formerly known as Theresienstadt. He intended to build a shopping mall, a *Platz*, there. Where heads were once shaved, where gold teeth were extracted, you'd be able to shop for the German equivalent of a Gap T-shirt and Caswell-Massey bath salts.

Civil war broke out in what used to be Yugoslavia, and there were rumors of genocide. A drunkard was in charge of Russia. The Romanians did a brisk trade in baby-selling, and Cardinal Glemp of Poland revived the time-honored tradition of Jew-bashing. That's the unsettling thing about this freedom business; when you've got choices, you run the risk of picking the wrong ones.

Lorraine had a baby boy. She named him Rudy. Lorraine

sang Soviet anthems to her child in lieu of lullabies, while her husband headed out to the tool shed with a pint of fortified wine.

Peter and his cross-eyed wife were sent to Brazil, where there are a lot of snakes, and the climate's not conducive to wearing a fox fur coat.

Some political scientists and economists were saying that the West Germans would regret the reunification. Absorbing the East Germans into the economy was proving to be a financial burden. But they, the experts, were forgetting the human factor. Once, some long years ago, Peter had told Lorraine and me the story of how after the war his mother carried him, a child then, across Czechoslovakia in a bathtub. A German needs to be united with other Germans at any cost, the same way a Southerner returns, like a homing pigeon, to Southern soil regardless of the price she has to pay. But a Jew, the Jew, ever wary, lives in an apartment building where there is no soil underfoot.

for widgit stands

That was the same year I had my father take down my closet door and hang beads in its place. I put up a poster of Janis Joplin on one wall and a macramé ornament on another. I was reading Herman Hesse, Kahlil Gibran, and *Jonathan Livingston Seagull*, which I thought to be deep, heady stuff. I wore a peace sign button on the lapel of my navy pea jacket. Heidi Rosenthal was my best friend.

Each night during Walter Cronkite, I braided my waist-length hair into cornrows, and in the morning I undid them. The result was hair that rippled down my back. I got the idea for rippled hair from Donna Huston, although her hair rippled naturally. Donna Huston was the most hippie girl in my grade, if not all of Hamilton Junior High. She could've been a centerfold for *Life* magazine with that hair, and the way her Sweet Orr bell-bottoms slid under the heels of her Fred Braun shoes. Her blouses were gauzy and made in India, land of many cool things like incense, the Maharishi, silver ankle bracelets with bells attached.

Appearances, however, sometimes deceived. In Social Studies class, when Mr. Tisch pulled down the map of the world and called on Donna Huston to point out Vietnam, she went looking for it in South America.

More than anything then, I yearned to be older than twelve going on thirteen. I wished I were old enough to sit-in, to strike, to protest and riot. It was with envy that I watched the film footage from the University of Michigan, of radicals chanting, "Hell no! We won't go!" and burning their draft cards and the American flag. Mounted police broke through the throngs of students. Placards went flying. Hippies ran for cover as the club-wielding cops bashed skulls, then handcuffed and tossed the hippies into the paddy wagon as if they were suitcases being loaded onto a conveyor belt.

Alas, by the time I was of age to hurl a bottle at a cop, it was all over.

After the report on the campus riot, Walter Cronkite had news from Vietnam. There were more casualties to report. I didn't think he should call dead people *casualties*. I thought he ought to say *dead people*. I imagined writing Walter Cronkite a letter to that effect, which he would read on the air. I went to sleep with the vision of Walter Cronkite holding up an envelope and telling America, "I have a letter here from a young girl . . ." Desperate for a way to protest, to make my voice heard, I hungered, not merely to enlist in the revolution, but to be the one with the bullhorn.

At school, during homeroom, Miss O'Connor, as she did every day, took attendance and then said, "All rise for the Pledge of Allegiance." In that instant it came to me, a flash of brilliance, the way to be the Mark Rudd, the Angela Davis, the Abbie Hoffman of the twelve-year-old set. I would boycott the Pledge. I would stand tall, but keep silent, a silence that would resonate from student to student, from homeroom to homeroom throughout the junior highs of America. What a day it would be when the teachers said, "All rise for the Pledge of Allegiance," and young people everywhere would stand up but clamp their mouths shut. That would be as cool as having a war but no one shows up to fight it.

Although I'd never have admitted it—not even to myself because I liked to think I'd have gladly done jail time for the cause—I took sly comfort knowing there'd be no serious repercussion over my boycott of the Pledge. Not that Miss O'Connor was in any way sympathetic to my politics, but there'd been some trouble in the past with Miss O'Connor requiring her homeroom to recite, along with the Pledge, the Lord's Prayer. My mother was president of the PTA that year and sat in on the meeting when some Jewish boy's parents made a stink about that. Miss O'Connor argued that the Lord's Prayer was nondenominational. "It's for all the religions and races," she said.

The Jewish boy's mother, a professor at Sarah Lawrence, wasn't swayed. "God doesn't belong in the public schools," she said, and she voiced concern for atheists and Zen Buddhists.

Miss O'Connor, who was best friends with the convent of nuns over at St. Eugene's, believed that God belonged everywhere, and atheists and whatnots deserved to have hot lead poured into their intestines. But she said none of that. Instead she said, "It's no different than having them recite the Pledge of Allegiance."

"Precisely," the Jewish boy's father agreed, "and they don't have to recite that either."

To avoid the possibility of a court case, the principal told Miss O'Connor the Lord's Prayer had to go, and no one had to recite anything they didn't want to recite. After the boy's parents left, the principal placated Miss O'Connor. "You know how the Jews get," he said.

And because Miss O'Connor already hated my guts—she hated all the hippies—I really had nothing to lose, although that didn't stop me from acting as if I did. Defiantly, I pinned my arms to my sides—no right hand draped over my heart— and I kept my mouth closed tightly while the class droned *I pledge allegiance to the flag mumble mumble America mumble for widgit stands,* and then a finger, Lydia Langorelli's finger to be exact, poked me in the back.

Lydia Langorelli had to repeat the third and fifth grades. Consequently, she was developed. While the rest of the girls in our class had rosebud breasts, Lydia had big hooters entombed in one of those old-fashioned conical cupped bras. She wore black eyeliner, Maybelline from Woolworth's, and nylon stockings with runs in them. She was not at all a hippie.

This was not the first time Lydia had poked me in the back. The week before she'd poked me and asked, "You got a comb?"

Of course I had a comb. Only I wasn't real keen on loaning it to Lydia Langorelli. But, I reminded myself, sharing property was an integral part of hippiedom, and so I fished out my comb from my fringed suede bag.

"Good." Lydia snatched it from me, and like it was a bowling trophy, she held up my faux mother-of-pearl comb and announced to the whole class, "Now I can clean out my hairbrush."

The boys laughed, and the girls cried, "Ewww, gross," as Lydia ran my comb through her filthy hairbrush, catching dandruff and grease and probably lice too.

A poke in the back from Lydia Langorelli was never going to be the best part of my day. Glumly I turned around to see what she wanted this time.

"The Pledge." She chomped on pink chewing gum. "We're saying the Pledge."

America right or wrong, love it or leave it, Lydia Langorelli was staunchly patriotic the way only the downtrodden could be. Lydia clung to the hope that if she pledged allegiance to the flag fervently enough, if tears sprung to her eyes during the national anthem, then someday America would do right by her. Thus far, America had dealt Lydia Langorelli dirt.

Although no one I knew had ever actually been there, it was common knowledge that Lydia lived in a shabby apartment over Pete's Pizza and Sub Shop where her father swept up and washed dishes for a living. When Lydia was just a little kid, her mother took off for a better life but turned up dead in a motel room in South Yonkers.

The rest of us at Hamilton Junior High lived in houses. Nice houses, and we had a plethora of luxuries to rebel against: charge accounts at Lord & Taylor, pink bedroom sets, country clubs that discriminated quietly. That we would eventually go off to college was a given.

I wasn't about to get into it—why I would not vow allegiance to a nation whose government was morally bereft—with Lydia Langorelli. She could never have grasped the concept of civil disobedience because to get left back twice you had to be a real moron. I turned my back on her *and justice for all*. As if we'd been standing at attention for hours, we, twenty-two seventh-graders, collapsed in our seats.

Again, Lydia's finger jabbed into my shoulder blade. "How come you didn't say the Pledge?" Obviously, she wasn't going to let the subject drop, so I gave her as succinct an answer as possible. While Lydia blew a large pink bubble, I explained, "It goes against my belief system."

Sucking the gum back into her mouth, Lydia said, "You don't believe in America? What are you? Some kind of Commie?" Then Lydia Langorelli told me, "After school. Today. I'm going to beat the shit out of you."

Beating the shit out of me was the one thing at which she was bound to excel. Those greaser girls were famous for biting, clawing, scratching, kicking, hair-pulling fights. And Lydia was the queen of the greasers. Not to mention she was twice my size. I didn't even know how to throw a punch. Violence was so uncool. I felt like I was going to throw up.

"Lydia Langorelli," Miss O'Connor's voice snapped like a whip. "Are you chewing gum? Get rid of that." Miss O'Connor quivered all over as if she were talking about something as nasty as a used condom instead of a wad of Bazooka.

Lydia spit the gum into her hand, but rather than wrapping it up in a piece of loose-leaf paper like you were supposed to, Lydia slapped her palm against the top of my head. She ground the pink gum into my hair.

My hair! My long, rippled, picture-of-the-young-hippie hair! Gum in my hair was so disastrous, I momentarily forgot that this wasn't going to be the worst of it.

When the bell rang, I met up with Heidi in the hall and showed her what Lydia'd done to me. "What can I do?"

Heidi seemed to remember hearing something about peanut butter as a chewing gum solvent. Or maybe it was margarine. "Either way," she said. "Go to Home Ec."

I nodded and then told her the rest. "She's going to beat me up after school."

Heidi gasped and clutched her books as if two notebooks and *The Red Pony* were a bulletproof vest. "Lydia Langorelli will kill you," Heidi said. "She'll mop the floor with you. You're dead meat." Seven years later, Heidi dropped out of college and joined the Church of Scientology.

Mrs. Rice, the orthopedic-shod dominatrix of the Home Ec rooms, reigned over six ovens, six double sinks, six refrigerators. Girls had to take Home Ec, where we made tuna casseroles and cinnamon toast. Boys took Shop. They got to build bookends and learn to use a blowtorch.

"How did this happen?" Mrs. Rice wanted to know how gum wound up in my hair, but I only shrugged because, no matter how egregious the crime, it wasn't cool to rat.

"Young ladies do not shrug their shoulders," Mrs. Rice reprimanded me, and before I knew what she was up to, she'd whipped a pair of scissors from her apron pocket and snipped. Mrs. Rice held up the wad of gum with two feet of my hair attached. It might as well have been a scalp Lydia Langorelli could've hung from her belt.

I stopped in the girls' room to assess the damage. A circle of hair, one inch in diameter, stood straight up on the top of my head like porcupine quills. Like a Hare Krishna in reverse.

Other than homeroom, Lydia was not in any of my classes because I was *accelerated* and she was *slow*. The only time I might've run into her during the day was at lunch. But I had no appetite, and instead of sliding my tray along in the cafeteria line, I went to hide out in Mr. Ellman's room.

I'd assumed Mr. Ellman would be eating his lunch in the faculty cafeteria, but there he was at his desk, munching granola and grading papers. Mr. Ellman was my English teacher. He had sort of long hair, and he referred to television as "the boob tube." Also, he let it be known he became a teacher because teachers got draft deferments.

"What's with your hair?" he asked. "Is that the latest in what's happening?"

"Yes," I said, and I half expected him to say *groovy*. But Mr. Ellman, embarrassed that he wasn't up on the newest hair trend, dropped the subject and asked, "What can I do for you?"

I pretended I'd come to talk to him about the war. He told me I should write letters to my congressman demanding troop withdrawal. I didn't know who my congressman was, but I didn't say anything about that. Nor did I say anything about Lydia Langorelli's plans to beat me to a bloody pulp. Not even when Mr. Ellman asked, "Are you okay? You look like something's bothering you." Mr. Ellman was the kind of teacher who liked kids to confide in him. Consequently, no one ever did.

"It's the war," I said. "Young men dying, getting maimed, and beat up. And for what? America? For which it stands?" My chin quivered, and I started to cry.

A man teacher could not hug me or pat me or dry my tears without courting disaster. One wrong move and Mr. Ellman would've found himself wading through the rice paddies.

Seventh period, I had Biology. While my lab partner hacked up an earthworm, dread danced in my stomach. I pictured myself sitting on the ground in the lotus position as Lydia licked me in the head. I tried to draw inspiration from Gandhi and Martin Luther King engaging in passive resistance. I was banking on passive resistance being a kind of invisible shield, whereby the blows inflicted wouldn't hurt much. I watched the clock on the wall, the red second hand sweeping around like it was in a hurry to get someplace. My hands went clammy.

Although I hadn't told anyone except Heidi that Lydia was going to beat me up after school, and I'd sworn her to secrecy, word had spread. When the bell rang, no one went home or to band practice or to cheerleading. Instead, two feet off of school property, the student body congregated in a circle. The air was crisp and smelled of burning leaves.

Lydia took off her leather jacket and gave it to some other greaser girl to hold. I handed my books to Heidi, and the cries went up, "Girl fight! Girl fight!" Then the crowd hushed so as not to miss the sound of Lydia's knuckles making contact with my face.

I heard the thwack, and I went down. My hands splayed behind me, so I wasn't flat out but sort of sitting. Lydia moved in and, as if to see if I were dead yet, she prodded me in the ribs with the point of her scuffed black shoe. I flinched and looked up at her, at her white lipstick, at the cheap sleeveless nylon shell she wore, at the pair of dunce caps she had for breasts, at the yellow discolorations on her arms that days before were purple and blue. And from someplace deep down where you know things you didn't think you knew, things you weren't supposed to know, much less ever talk about, *I knew*. I knew, and I said, "You have sex with your father."

As if I'd decked her in a soft and tender place, her eyes bugged from the unexpected low blow and then swirled into a kaleidoscope of pain and fear. Suddenly, she was the prey, as stunned as the cobra who thought the mongoose just another rodent. She mouthed the word *no*, but instead of a rush of compassion, I experienced a rush of adrenaline. Fueled by victory, crazed by power, I got up and shrieked at the top of my lungs for the whole school to hear, "Lydia Langorelli fucks her father. She gives him blow jobs and cooks him spaghetti."

The crowd was with me now; they were mine. Everyone, including the girl holding Lydia's leather jacket, hooted and laughed and whistled because this unexpected turn of events was far more inspiring than merely watching Lydia beat the shit out of me. Besides, Lydia was just some greaser who'd been left back twice. And no one, no one in the whole *I pledge allegiance to the flag of the United States of America* gave a widgit about Lydia Langorelli.

money honey

My father, his sisters, his brother, and his cousins have congregated in the living room to eat cheese Danish, drink coffee laced with cream and NutraSweet, and to try to figure out a way—legal, mind you—to swindle their uncle Max out of his share of the inheritance. I'm here because I've recently left my husband and haven't, for the moment, anyplace else to go. My uncle Marty's son, Alex, a third-year law student at Cardozo, is giving counsel. I take a swallow of wine and wonder if Alex has ever been with a woman.

Here's the situation: My great-uncle Jack died and left a mattress full of money to no one in particular. This money comes to the tune of two point nine four million dollars; not an amount to sneeze at. Everyone in the family knew that

Jack had some money because he made a decent living and never spent five cents. But who knew it was that much money; not even my aunt Pauline knew, and Pauline made it her business to be concerned with Jack's finances.

Pauline believes she is most deserving of whatever money Jack had to leave behind because she's had the most miserable life in the family. A little money would help ease her sorrows. The sorrows of Pauline are often retold at family get-togethers and usually by Pauline herself, as if she can't get enough of the story about her husband, a gambler who took up with a dancer and left Pauline and the twins without so much as a dollar. Pauline was forced to go to work, to work her fingers to the bone to feed and clothe the twins, who grew up to be a pair of ingrates. Just like their father, they left Pauline as soon as they could get away and never call to say so much as hello.

And if that wasn't enough misery for any one person— Pauline finally met a nice man with whom she kept company. For seven years, she cooked him dinner and pressed his undershorts, when he upped and decided there were other fish in the sea. From Aunt Pauline's life story, I concluded that men aren't so interested in having their underwear ironed.

I come from a family of rejects; I'm the first one that anyone can remember who was the jilter as opposed to the jilted. When I walked out on Bernie seven weeks ago, my aunt Esther said, "You got Ruth's genes."

"That's not possible, Aunt Esther," I said. "Ruth wasn't a blood relative."

Ruth was Louie's wife. In 1954, when she was forty-five, she ran off with the butcher, never to be heard from again. Even though she was long gone before I was born, she is my favorite aunt. I'm the only one in the family who doesn't make a spitting gesture when her name is mentioned. "How could she have left two little boys like that? It's unnatural for a mother to leave her children." Never mind that her two little boys, Cecil and Stanley, were grown men with wives of their own when their mother fell in love and decided to do something about it. Cecil's wife, in 1967, joined a commune in Vermont and divorced him by walking around a chicken three times under a full moon.

"No one on our side of the family," Esther said to me, "walks out on a marriage. Now go back to your husband."

FOR SEVERAL WEEKS, Pauline refused to accept that Jack had not drawn up a will. She went through Jack's apartment slashing canvas, tapping at walls, leaving no stone unturned. There had to be a will somewhere because Pauline was certain that Jack had bequeathed his money to her. "I was the only one who gave a damn about him," she says. Pauline used to call Uncle Jack once a week to see if he was dead yet. "To check on his health" was the way she put it.

There is a procedure for distributing the goods in the absence of a will, and the first step is this: the money gets divided equally among his three brothers. Two of these three brothers are dead. One of the dead ones would have been my grandfather if he hadn't been knocked down and killed by a runaway milk truck when my father was still a boy. The other dead brother was Louie, the one Ruth ran out on. He drowned in the surf at Coney Island in 1962. Therefore Louie's sons, Cecil and Stanley, get to split his third of the inheritance just as my father, Pauline, Esther, and Marty will divide their father's share four ways. My father, Pauline, Esther, and Marty are now wishing heart attacks on each other.

The big winner in this jackpot is Uncle Max, the third brother and the one who is still among the breathing. He gets to keep his share all for himself. Max married for the first time some nine years before when he was seventy-three. He married Shirley, a widow with three grown children and a multitude of grandchildren, whom he met at the Morris Park Senior Center.

"I was Jack's favorite," Pauline says, lighting up her third Winston 100 in a row. Pauline is a chain-smoker who has polyps on her throat and a whopping smoker's cough.

No one pays any attention to Pauline's griping. Their bone of contention is Max, who, as they see it, does not deserve all this money. He didn't like Jack any better than the others did.

"I called Jack once a week," Pauline repeats. "Toll calls. That ought to be worth something."

"Aunt Pauline," Marty's boy, Alex, says, "you can't get reimbursed for the phone calls now."

"Which," Marty pipes in, "you only made in the first place trying to get into Jack's good graces. Hah!"

"People, people." Stanley motions for everyone to settle

down, to focus on the issue at hand. "Max is an old man," he reasons. "What is an old man going to do with that kind of money? I've got kids in college. Private college. Do you have any idea what that costs these days?"

"The point is," my father says, "now that Max has got a wife, what if she should divorce him? Half that money would go to her and then to her children by a previous marriage to a stranger. The money should not leave the family," my father says, as if this cash has great sentimental value.

For our second wedding anniversary, Bernie gave me money. One thousand dollars. Ten spanking new $100 bills in an envelope. He said, "For you. To get yourself whatever you want. Happy anniversary."

Along with some onions, tomatoes, lemon peel, mint, and parsley, I put the $1,000 in the food processor and diced and minced and then mixed all of it together with couscous. I didn't tell Bernie that he'd eaten his money until two nights later, after he'd climbed off me in bed.

I get up for more wine. My mother is in the kitchen putting up a fresh pot of coffee. "You should go easy on that, maybe," she says as I refill my glass.

"And listen to that stone-cold sober?" I cock my head toward the living room.

My mother turns away from all of it, and I settle back into the sofa as my father is saying, "Look, we'll explain it to him. He'll understand."

"Sure," Esther says. "Max is going to give us a million dollars because it's the reasonable thing to do."

Earlier in the day, Esther had showed me a list she'd

written outlining how she was going to spend her pile of money. Esther wants to buy a fur coat—fox or mink, she hasn't yet made up her mind; she wants to take a trip to Hawaii; and she wants box seats for the opera. I told Aunt Esther that her list was very nice, which must have given her the impression that she and I could talk. Esther sat herself down next to me and pulled me to her in a motherly fashion. "Now," she said, "when are you going to quit acting like a spoiled little girl? Do you know what you're doing to your parents? Go back to Bernie. Make everyone happy."

"I don't love Bernie, Aunt Esther." I eased myself from her clutches.

"So? What's that got to do with anything? Love." Esther made a face as if she were smelling fish. "Look where love got Pauline. Who needs that? Bernie gave you a comfortable life. Be grateful for that."

The night I left Bernie, Aunt Esther, who can smell trouble from two blocks away, came rushing over, a coat thrown over her nightgown, to join in the discussion. It was just after midnight and all I wanted to do was go to sleep, but the three of them, my parents and Esther, demanded an explanation, a way to understand: Does he hit you? Does he drink? Does he gamble? He provides nicely for you? You got out for dinner often?

"He's terrible in bed," I said, and my father left the room. "And he's getting fat. He's only twenty-eight and already he's got a spare tire. I'm not attracted to him."

"There's more than that to making a marriage." My

mother lives to compromise. "So he's a little chubby. More of him to love."

"But I don't love him at all," I said, and Esther said, "She's got Ruth's genes."

MY COUSIN ALEX, Marty's boy, is showing himself to be a sleazeball. He's come up with the idea of having Max declared incompetent. "And then one of us gets power of attorney and handles his money accordingly."

"Us?" I ask Alex. "What's with this *us* business? None of this money is yours, is it?"

Alex goes red in the face and he stammers, "I mean, those, the people I'm representing."

"Representing now, are we? Practicing law without a license. Doesn't the bar have some funny little rule about that?"

"Don't pay any attention to her," my father says. "A woman who leaves her husband . . ." The rest of his words get stuck in his throat, and he waves his hand as if I were piffle.

"Besides," Marty adds, "she's been drinking."

MY MOTHER SITS at the kitchen table looking worried or sad, maybe. She is picking walnuts off a coffee cake and eating them without pleasure. "Don't," she says to me, and I ask, "Don't what? Do you hear what's going on out there? They're like jackals."

"Shh," my mother hushes me. "Your own family. You shouldn't talk like that."

My own family. People who equate love with obligation, who tell me I have to settle. My own family treats me now like I'm from the other side. I suppose I am. From the other side. Closer in kind to the wayward in-laws. "*I* shouldn't talk like that?"

Before I can say anything else, my mother clamps her hands over her ears. If she had another set of hands, she would use them to cover her eyes. As is, she turns away when I open a fresh bottle of wine. Last night, my mother sat by my side and said, "Maybe love isn't what you thought it would be. Maybe it's not Bernie who isn't so hot. How would you know from how it's supposed to be?"

My mother wasn't ready for my answer. No one is ever ready to hear what they don't want to know. There is no good time to tell your mother that you've had more lovers than she can count, and there is no good time to dump your husband. "That's enough," my mother said, and she went and locked herself in the bathroom.

Now I think about coming to Uncle Max's rescue. Standing strong beside him. I picture the courtroom: all the relatives on one side, pop-eyed with greed; Max and I fighting for truth and justice, which really is not the American way. Still, I'd prove to the jury that Max is as competent as they are, and that his nieces and nephews are trying to cheat the dead and the elderly. I must've watched a scene like this in a movie because the truth is, I don't know if that would've come to me on my own. I don't know that I care about Uncle Max any more than I care about any of my other relatives. Max has extremely large ears, like the kind Lyndon Johnson had, but Max's ears are practically useless. When Marty called Uncle Max to tell him that Jack had died, Max said, "What? What?" Max is deaf enough not to hear himself pass gas. He doesn't hear it so he assumes no one else hears it. I really wouldn't want to spend more time with Uncle Max than I have to, no matter what the circumstances.

It's just that my indignation evens up the score.

They tell me that not only have I broken Bernie's heart, but I have done something warped and shameful: I walked out on a perfectly good marriage.

Never mind that if it were a perfectly good marriage, I wouldn't have walked out on it.

My parents adore Bernie. My father says Bernie is the son he didn't have. My mother calls Bernie a prince, a king. He is everything they could have wanted for me.

Bernie is a marshmallow. He wouldn't have thrown me out no matter what I did to provoke him. I had to leave him because I couldn't get him to leave me. During the two and a half years of marriage to Bernie, I had four affairs. One with an old boyfriend of mine, another with a man I met at a party who wrote down his phone number on a paper napkin that he gave to me along with a shrimp on a toothpick. There was a fling with the man who fixed my car at the garage, and then there was the string of afternoons with one of the partners at Bernie's firm, so, yeah, I suppose you could say his boss.

Well, at least I wouldn't try to swindle an old man out of a little bit of money.

"Why did you marry me in the first place?" Bernie asked, and I said, "Bernie, that is a question I ask myself every single day."

THEY ARE ALL hot on the idea of having Max declared incompetent. What they are trying to do now is come up with stories about him, stories that will establish him as unable to act in his own self-interests. This is not so easy. Not only does Max have all his faculties up and running, he isn't even eccentric. Their stories—once he got lost at a flea market, he can't hear a thing, he eats fruit without washing it, he's deaf as a post, he, pardon my French, expels gas in mixed company, did we mention that he's deaf?—these are feeble and prove nothing but their desperation. Pity they didn't come up with this idea while Jack was alive. With Jack, they might have had a case. A millionaire three times over who lived in a nearly condemned building, a recluse. They could've channeled Jack through the courts and into Bellevue.

I find myself wishing that Jack had willed his money to a pet canary.

With one cigarette still burning in the ashtray, Pauline lights another and says, "There was that time he wandered out of Elaine's wedding and sat down to dinner at a bar mitzvah in the next hall."

"You people are not to be believed," I say.

"And I suppose," my father says to me, "if someone were going to give you money, you would refuse it?"

"I fail to make the connection. No one is giving you anything," I point out. "You're stealing."

"You send her off to that fancy college," Pauline says, "and look how she turns out."

There is a physical resemblance between Pauline and me. Around the eyes and the mouth. I look like I could be Pauline's daughter. It's always said that Pauline was the beauty in the family until bitterness and cigarettes and overeating won out. I wonder how many affairs her husband had before he took off with the dancer.

I'm tipsy enough that I start thinking about seducing Marty's boy, my cousin Alex.

When Bernie and I started dating, he was a virgin. I don't think I ever forgave him for that. I thought it to be a defect, and I pitied him for it. The sort of pity that mushrooms into disgust.

On the coffee table in the living room, my mother puts down a tray of sandwiches—turkey, Swiss cheese, tuna. No one thanks my mother for the food, but they do make a beeline for it. Talking with their mouths full, they claim they are too upset to eat.

My mother joins me on the sofa and says to me, "I know it looks like they're not being very nice. But try and see it from their side. No one has had an easy life. It's not right that you sit here criticizing."

"Getting more money isn't going to make them happy," I say.

"And what about you?" my mother asks. "What will it take to make you happy?"

Seven weeks ago, Bernie was on top of me, his eyes closed, his mouth hanging open like a dufus, pumping away, and I said, "Bernie, when you're done here, I'm leaving you."

Marty wants to know if anyone has spoken to Max about a will. "If he's careful about what he leaves to who and provided he doesn't go crazy on some kind of spending spree, we could come into it when, God forbid, he passes on."

The telephone rings and my mother goes to the kitchen to answer it. At first, when I left him, Bernie was calling here twice a day. I refused to speak to him, so he talked to my mother and to my father, asking them to relay messages, messages requesting that I come to my senses and return to him. Bernie conspired with *my* family, which I didn't think was fair.

My mother signals for me to come into the kitchen. She is holding the phone out to me and she says, "It's Bernie. Go on, talk to him. It couldn't hurt just to talk."

I take the phone, and I say hello and Bernie says, "I'm filing for divorce."

"That's a good plan," I tell him.

"I'm filing for divorce on the grounds of adultery."

"Yeah, well, that's fair."

"You're not going to get anything from me." Bernie's voice breaks. "Do you understand that? Nothing. No settlement. No alimony. Not the house. Not the furniture. Not the food processor. Not the coffeemaker." He's cracking up. "I won't give you a penny. You'll pay for this. I want you to suffer. Do you hear me? Suffer." Bernie does not wait for me to respond. He hangs up on me.

I keep the phone next to my ear, listening to the dial tone for a while, and I return to the living room just as my aunt Pauline says, "I have nothing. I should at least have some money."

I

She showed me how to paint light. Imagine. Painting light. A dab of white dotting the clown's nose and presto! a reflection. A streak of yellow breaking up a cloud, and I got light like God coming to Moses in my book titled *Bible Stories*. Light. This was no small accomplishment. Painting light. Then she said to me, "I'm sure the other children are very nice, but they are inferior to you. Remember that."

Aside from how to create light, aside from that I was superior to the other kids, she instructed I keep a good address. "She's *meshuga*," my father said. "Sleeps on an army cot. No food in the cupboards. But on Riverside Drive, yet."

There was food, though. She ate sardines and crackers.

Sardines packed neatly in their cans. Clever little fish fitting together just so. Like a puzzle. Or a trick with mirrors. A single fish reflected twelve times.

Oh, there was one other thing she said. "Never, ever disturb a bird's nest," she told me, "because if you do, the birds will abandon it."

II

Drop-dead gorgeous. Exotic in junior furs. Sweaters by Oleg Cassini. Add-A-Pearl necklaces by Tiffany's completed for sweet sixteens. Ambitions by mothers, and if not graced by God's light touch, then by Dr. Diamond's scalpel. Dr. Diamond, the nose-job king. Pink-frosted lipstick. Frosted hair. Frosted nails. Frost like a fine layer of ice. Such glamorous dolls, we were Social Darwinism in action. The mean-spiritedness was nothing more than acts of omission.

Once, a short and plump boy threw an egg at Marcia. It landed squarely on her chest. Splatted on off-white cashmere, and it made Marcia cry. When the rest of us confronted him, demanding to know what the fuck his problem was, he went red with rage. "All of you. You look at me like I'm not there."

"So what?" Bev said. "We look at everyone like they're not there."

Even each other. Even ourselves. And I considered myself blessed to be included, to break bread at their lunch table.

III

Before Yeltsin, before Gorbachev, before sporting Cyrillic T-shirts was all the rage, Nancy shaved off her eyebrows. With food coloring meant for cupcake frosting, she dyed her white cat red and took up smoking cigarettes through an amber holder. Next, she said, "I'm to be called Natasha now," and she joined the Russian Orthodox Church, the one on the Upper East Side.

After the Easter service, an all-night affair without so much as a bathroom break, they rejoiced over breakfast, a buffet of treats imported from the motherland. Taking advantage of the inherent sensuality of fish eggs, Natasha made a sexual suggestion to a bearded and brooding priest. Tongues wagged Russian style, and so Natasha converted.

This time she became an Episcopalian. Read Barbara Pym novels and asked the vicar in for tea. Over Earl Grey, scones with jam, and cucumber sandwiches, the vicar described for her his collection of Fiesta ware. He had the complete set in red. Nancy would've blown the pope for a full set of red Fiesta ware. She set her sights on this vicar, on becoming his wife, on joint custody of the dishes. She talked much of this, and of the good work she'd do with the gentlewomen—which is English for "bag ladies"—as the clergyman's wife.

The vicar came to tea again, and the two of them waxed ecstatic over cobalt glass, ruby glass, crystal cut so all colors of the spectrum reflect, refract, onto a white linen tablecloth.

On his third afternoon to tea, the vicar left Nancy's apartment not long before dawn. When he stepped out onto the street to hail a cab back to the rectory, hoping to get there before the others awoke, he was knocked down, killed, by a garbage truck making early-morning rounds.

For Nancy, there were no churches left. She'd been through them all.

IV

Ann's ancestors were Plain. Not Amish, although something like that. They wore somber colors. No buttons or jewelry. Laughter was the devil's voice. They didn't dance either.

But Ann was not at all like her grandmothers. Ann was self-indulgent. She wore makeup, bracelets, hair ribbons, the works. She considered herself to be wild even though she was thirty years old and still lived, along with four brothers, at home with her parents. Theirs was a square house on a tree-lined block in a part of Brooklyn like no other part of Brooklyn, an enclave cut off from mass transit. With her family lived three dogs and a cat. One dog was deaf, another blinded by glaucoma. The third dog had only two legs. The cat, too, was blind. Its eyes were missing. Each animal's story ended with Ann's family offering refuge, an act of charity.

It was that sort of thing, an act of charity, that prompted me to offer Ann my apartment for the summer I was away. Privacy was a gift she needed. "Make yourself at home," I said.

She made herself at home. Entirely at home. When I returned, I found my furniture rearranged. My paintings were taken down and stacked in a closet. Only the nails jutting out from the walls remained as testimony that something had once hung there. A pair of silver earrings had vanished along with my Add-A-Pearl necklace, two silk camisoles, and a pair of fishnet stockings.

But the baffling question remains: Why did she cut out the elastic from the fitted sheets?

When I asked, she went mute. Rocked in her high-backed chair like Norman Bates as his mother, denying it all.

V

There are no coincidences. That Bev and I should meet while waiting for the light to change at Third Avenue and Forty-sixth Street was a miracle. But troubling. I hadn't seen her in ten or eleven years, and there she was, wearing a floral print dress with a white, scalloped collar. She had Reeboks on her feet and one of those papoose thingies strapped to her back. There was a baby in it. Its head and arms and legs stuck out like a pithed frog. It drooled on her Lord & Taylor dress, and I couldn't fathom how it got there.

Prior to this meeting, the last time I'd seen Bev was the night before we went off to college, our separate ways. We'd dropped quaaludes, and consequently, everything was funny. We got so silly that we even talked about our lives, about what we wanted, what we'd get. "I know I'm supposed to grow as a person," Bev said, "but honestly, I can't see it happening." We stretched out our legs on her blue shag carpet, and I told her

I didn't think I'd ever get married because I couldn't imagine it. This we thought so hilarious that Bev peed. Perhaps it was sitting in the puddle that sobered her. "You are so fucking weird," she said.

Now, she talked about her new name, which was Shapiro, and about her co-op, and about her upcoming vacation to Puerto Rico. Finally I said, "Is that yours?" meaning the baby. Only it came out like I was referring to something that had fallen to the ground, a piece of paper or a scarf, maybe.

"Don't you have children?" she asked.

At first, I didn't understand the question. Then, I shook my head and explained, "I'm very immature for my age."

VI

As if I could be a band of Israeli commandos, and the Entebbe airport were a mobile home someplace awful, I wanted to swoop down and rescue her. Save her from yet another stupid mistake.

The last time I tried saving her, I couldn't. And she hit bottom, from which she did not bounce back like the clean and swift rebound on a trampoline. Rather, she crawled her way out, grabbing hold of dirt and twigs. Afterward, she said to me, "I appreciated your effort, but you can't stop a natural disaster. It's not possible. Don't even try."

I did learn one other thing. One she does not know about: Just because she is gone, I do not also disappear.

This past February, she came back to town to collect the

rest of her things from storage. Nice Jewish Boys Moving and Storage Company. She always put her things in safekeeping with Nice Jewish Boys. "Your people," she'd say to me.

I helped her pack up, and then we went for dinner to one of those Cuban-Chinese joints on Eighth Avenue. We ate *pollo frito* and plantains. Sweet plantains. It was snowing when I walked her to her car. Under a streetlamp we stood, snowflakes landing on her eyelashes, lingering for only an instant before melting away. "Please," she said, "don't abandon me."

in the beginning

First came the Yettas, the Sophies, shuttled by boat from one ghetto to another. In the sweatshops, which were firetraps, Sophie and Yetta hunched over the sewing machines and worked themselves half to death. Then they got married and worked the other half of themselves to death. Keeping a kosher home, in and of itself, was a full-time job. Shopping daily, first to the butcher—that *gonif* you had to watch like a hawk because his thumb had a habit of resting on the scale alongside the roast. Next to the greengrocer, the baker, and home up five flights of stairs to wait for the ice-man, who made improper advances. On Friday nights, Yetta and Sophie lit *Shabbes* candles, which was almost as much of a pleasure as skimming the cream from the milk to give to their children.

Their children were daughters: Shirley, Sylvia, Muriel. Cigarette-smoking, throaty-voiced, bleached blondes. They learned a trade, became bookkeepers or real estate agents until marrying schmucks named Sy, Morris, Hymie. Then, they got the hell out of the city, moved to the suburbs where they joined the local temple. No longer called *shul*, or even *synagogue*, but *temple*. It was more of a social thing—dinner dances, the theater group, fund-raising for the starving in Israel. In their own homes, Shirley, Sylvia, Muriel, didn't keep kosher. Who had the time what with Hadassah meetings and schlepping the kids to piano lessons and ballet class? This eating of *trayf* wasn't given a second thought except to say of their own mothers, "She worked her fingers to the bone keeping kosher and never even knew for what. So ignorant." While Shirley, Sylvia, Muriel, never learned the reasons for the two sets of dishes either, they weren't so ignorant as to slave for what was beyond them. In fact, they weren't about to slave at all and so got a girl to come on Saturdays to do the heavy cleaning.

Shirley, Sylvia, Muriel, begot Mindy, Marcy, Renée. Occasionally, a Mindy went haywire and joined the Hare Krishnas or took to *shtupping* black men. Mostly, though, they were carbon copies of their own mothers except they played tennis at the club instead of canasta. Also, they had small, upturned noses, *shiksa* noses, because, thank God, their fathers did well enough to afford the best plastic surgeon and not some butcher. Mindy, Marcy, Renée, married Howard, a

CPA, Michael, who will take over his father's jewelry business, and Richard, a doctor, a specialist in urology.

These couples return to the faith when it comes to naming their own children. Their boys are called Joshua, Samuel, Max. The girls got names like Shulamith, Rebecca, Ariel.

Ariel goes to a school for intellectually gifted children. On a class trip to Ellis Island, she sees pictures of immigrants getting off boats. Ariel opens her tiny Fendi purse, takes out a blue crayon, and defaces the photograph of Yetta.

This is the third time in as many weeks that Marcy gets a phone call from the school regarding Ariel's behavior problem.

carlotta

The child I do not have is named Carlotta. She is six years old, in the first grade. I need Carlotta to be of school age, but I want her to be young enough still to have small hands; pocket-sized wonders of anatomy. Carlotta has big brown eyes and cappuccino-colored skin. It's not clear to me whether Carlotta will grow into a great beauty. On her ears, she wears gold filigree rings.

At twenty minutes before three o'clock, I would go out and walk to the school Carlotta attends. Many mothers and a few fathers are there waiting for their children. Also, a number of Jamaican nannies dressed in bright and mismatched colors have come to meet their blond charges. I might smile, nod in greeting at some of these parents and guardians, but I would not join in the conversations. When the school bell rings, and the children surge like floodwaters from the doors, Carlotta would find me leaning against the wall smoking a cigarette.

"Sylvie," she says, as if she weren't quite sure I'd show up. Her nylon knapsack slung over her shoulder, Carlotta slips one hand into mine. Involuntarily, as if my hand were my heart pumping, I squeeze Carlotta's wondrous little hand in greeting, thump, thump, thump.

We would walk for two blocks to our favorite café where I would order an espresso for myself. Carlotta would get a baba au rhum and spumoni. I let her have two desserts because I don't believe in saying no. While she eats, alternating bites of each sweet, Carlotta would tell me about her day at school, about the numbers she's mastered, about the story she read in her primer—a hokey story. Carlotta prefers the stories I read to her, the fairy tales unedited. She particularly goes for "Cinderella," lapping up the part where the stepsisters hack off pieces of their own feet. That day, Carlotta would also have had music class. Carlotta makes a face. She doesn't think much of her music teacher. I picture Carlotta's music teacher to be much like the music teacher I had in the first grade, a crabby, white-haired woman with a pitch pipe. Carlotta's music teacher doesn't allow Carlotta to sway with the beat but demands she stand straight and tall while singing. "She yelled at me again for dancing," Carlotta tells me, and I tell Carlotta, "The woman is frustrated. Try to understand what that does to a person."

Carlotta laughs and licks her spoon. A rush of love

comes over me the way embarrassment does, and I wonder if I'm blushing.

Next, I picture Richard coming into the café where I sit with Carlotta. I am consumed with love for Richard, although I'd be hard-pressed to explain why. He is sick with love for me too, but he's married someone named Claire. I've never met Claire, but I picture her to be a crisp woman whose clothes never wrinkle.

Richard tortures himself with questions of morality and fear of consequences. The man does not dare; he is a coward. Only when he gets to our table does Richard see Carlotta. "Well, who's this?" he asks in one of those voices people use when talking to children, dogs, and the elderly.

"This is Carlotta," I introduce them, the two people I love, to each other.

Carlotta, wise beyond her years, would then ask if she could move to another table, by herself, to sit alone. "I'd like to draw pictures, and this table is too busy," she'd say.

Whenever she has the opportunity, Carlotta draws pictures. Blank paper is an irresistible force for the child I do not have. Her homework would sport ornate panels for margins, and at home she doodles on the walls with Magic Markers. Carlotta favors drawing trees and flowers and jungles with parrots half-hidden by foliage. She would not draw the box houses and stick figures and shining yellow sun that most children pass off as art. Carlotta's work has a Gauguin-ish quality to it.

I would like it if Carlotta grew up to become an artist,

painting huge canvases with swirls of colors with names like crimson lake, cerulean blue, hooker's green, and rose madder genuine. Painters, generally, are happy people. I never imagine Carlotta becoming a poet. Poets are a morose group of drunks who all too often wind up in despair jumping from bridges into icy waters. And I do admit I'd be devastated if one day she came to me and said, "Sylvie, I want to be an actress." I can't stomach actresses, all breathy and stupid. Of course, when you have children, you have to let them go in their own direction; a downside I don't have to deal with. Carlotta will become a painter, and already at the age of six, she shows great promise.

At a table by herself, one where I can keep an eye on her, Carlotta unzips her knapsack and takes out her art supplies, drawing paper and a box of oil-based pastels. She is hunched over, intent on her work while Richard and I talk. Initially, Richard and I talk of nothing much, maybe so desperate as to remark on the weather but, as is our way, this banal chitchat will lead to something. I might say, "It would be good, us together." However, Richard would rather be an upstanding member of society than happy in the end. "Oh, Sylvie. How? How could we manage? It's not possible. We shouldn't even talk about it. I have responsibilities," he says.

"Don't we all," I could say, meaning Carlotta.

At some point, this talk would be interrupted because Carlotta would come over to us. She'd be carrying a sheet of paper by the tip of one corner so as not to smudge anything.

She places her art on the table for me to see. Carlotta has drawn a garden, lush with pink hibiscus and deep green leaves. There is no sky. "Carlotta," I say, "we must frame this when we get home."

Richard would twist in his seat to get a better view. "That's really good," he'd say. "Amazing, in fact," and Carlotta, a generous child, gives it to him. "It's for you," she says. She has one foot behind the other, and she looks bashful.

Because there'd be no way for him to explain to his wife how he came to have a pastel drawing of a lush garden, he and I both know he will throw it in a trash can when he leaves the café. To assuage the guilt of conscience this—crumpling up and abandoning a gift of love—generates, Richard would take five dollars from his wallet and tell Carlotta, "In the real world, art is a commodity to be purchased." Carlotta wouldn't know what the hell he was talking about, so he'd clarify, "I won't let you give it to me, but I will buy it from you."

As that, quid pro quo, is the only way Richard knows how to give and take, I tell Carlotta yes, she should take the money. Then, Richard offers her a stick of gum, spearmint, which Carlotta snaps up.

"Now, Carlotta," I remind her of her manners, "what do bourgeois people expect you to say when they give you something?"

"Thank you," Carlotta singsongs. "Thank you very much."

The child I do not have would then return to her table to make another picture, and Richard would say to me, "She's lovely."

"Yes," I'd agree, as pleased and proud as if she really were my child, as if I'd given birth to her, which is not something I can even properly imagine. The image of me pregnant is always a fleeting one. I can't tolerate so much as the concept of growing fat, of becoming one of those women who serenely rub their expanding belly the way you rub a bald man's head for luck. Stretch marks, hemorrhoids, swollen ankles, flatulence, all the unpleasantries associated with pregnancy, would sadden me. I do not wish to lactate, not ever. Nor would I have wanted the infant Carlotta around because I wouldn't know what to do with an infant, and I wouldn't want to learn. Carlotta is six years old because I could never, not even in a daydream, bring myself to change a diaper. Therefore, the child I do not have has come to me walking, talking, toilet-trained, and able to blow her own nose. Carlotta is a foster child. Her mother, her birth mother, could either be in jail or a hopeless crack addict.

Richard has two children. Real ones. A boy and a girl. The boy is a year younger than Carlotta. The girl is new to the world. She is still a sniveling little blob of pink skin and cartilage, unable even to sit up yet; never mind capable of drawing gardens of pink hibiscus the way Carlotta can.

Those two children are the excuse Richard gives me for not leaving his wife. "I have a family," he says. "I have obligations. What about my children? You can't just walk out on kids."

Although I'm not really keen on the idea, I tell him, "They can live with us." I call Carlotta over and ask her, "Carlotta, would you like to run off with Richard and me? We could run off to Paris. Would you like that?"

Carlotta claps her hands together and gasps, "Oh, yes, Sylvie. Yes." Carlotta would adore living in Paris. She could carry one of those French schoolbags instead of that dreadful knapsack. She'd wear a pleated skirt, white knee socks, and a beret at a jaunty angle. After school, she and I would go to a patisserie for café au lait and petits fours.

But I can also see Richard shaking his head. "You try to simplify what's complicated, Sylvie. You talk as if we were the only two people in the world, that we can go around doing whatever we want. But there is so much more to consider. Love," he says, "is not justification enough to go off wrecking families and careers and other people's lives. Be sensible. I've got a mortgage."

Sometimes, love doesn't count for anything at all.

Sometimes, when I think about Carlotta, I also think about her mother getting sprung from jail or rehab, and how she'd want Carlotta back. And I wouldn't have any choice in the matter. A judge would order me to return Carlotta as if she were a library book I'd borrowed. But I don't think about that for long. I'd much rather think about Carlotta and me walking home from the café. "He's nice," Carlotta would say about Richard, and I would correct her.

"No, Carlotta," I'd say. "He's pathetic. Don't mistake weakness for kindness."

Skipping alongside me, Carlotta would take that in, understand in ways, perhaps, that even I did not. Then, I'd ask her what would she like for dinner—pizza or Chinese food?—because I don't like to cook and Carlotta, she's wild about eating off paper plates.

AUGUST 2
Chase City, Virginia

At the Chase City Goodwill Store, Lorraine looks for clothes for her child and blouses for herself. I busy myself at the hat rack, where I find two synthetic wigs. I bring them to Lorraine and say, "Look. A buck apiece. We can't go wrong."

Lorraine and I are not well. Her sickness is in her head. She's been neglecting her personal hygiene. Also, her hair is dyed blond, which doesn't become her.

The wig Lorraine chooses is flame-red, the same color her hair was when she lived in New York. My wig is as black as bile.

Lorraine, wearing her wig, pushes Rudy in his stroller up the steep hill, and she asks me, "Do you think this sort of thing, the wig, will scandalize them?" By *them*, Lorraine means the fine people of Chase City. She has applied for membership to the Chase City Country Club. When she first applied for club membership, she worried that they might have a gentleman's agreement or an outright policy: No Jews Allowed. "It was a dilemma," she told me. "What with you being my best friend. What if you came to visit and they wouldn't let you in? But then I remembered you don't swim or play golf, so what would it matter?"

I tell Lorraine she need not worry about scandalizing the neighbors. "Wig or no wig, they're not going to let you into their country club."

We stop at Judy's Beauty Salon because Lorraine wants to ask about dyeing her hair another color from the blond she's got now. She is less depressed because I am here. Three women sit under helmet dryers, the sort of dryers I haven't seen for years. Judy, a dumpy honey-blonde without a hint of panache, is horrified at the sight of Lorraine. "Is that a wig you've got on?" she asks.

"Yes," Lorraine tells her.

"Thank the Lord." The beautician's hand goes to her heart.

"But what I want to know," Lorraine asks, "is if you can make my hair like this? This color and style?" The wig is not only red, but the acrylic hair is short, Gigi-esque. In Chase City, long blond hair cut in a shag is the cat's meow.

Judy says, "Now, honey. You don't really want that," and I take Lorraine by the arm. "Let's go home," I say, and we return to Lorraine's house.

Lorraine's mother bought this house for her. Before that,

she lived in a trailer in a town called Dillwyn with her husband and child. "You can't go on like this. You can't live in a trailer," her mother had said. Having taken every precaution to ensure that Lorraine would not wind up with a gun-toting, cap-wearing, good ol' boy for a husband, her mother's worst nightmare was realized when Lorraine married Mac. Looking to remedy the situation, her mother said, "I'll buy you a house. A nice house, but he can't live in it. I'm not buying him a house."

The attachment to the soil, a plot of Southern land that Lorraine could call her own, was greater than her attachment to Mac. She and Rudy now live on Sycamore Street in a nice white house with evergreen shutters and a front porch.

In Lorraine's bedroom, I take my wig from the bag and try it on. It fits snugly on my head, and Lorraine remarks on how I look like a young Liz Taylor. "Only with brown eyes."

We head out to the porch. I sit on the swing. Lorraine surveys the street from the white wicker chair. She is still hurt that short, red hair didn't go over big at the beauty parlor.

No matter that she was born here, that her parents and grandparents and generations of ancestors before them were born, lived, and died in this state, in this county, Lorraine doesn't belong. "They don't get you here," I say.

"They don't get anything here," Lorraine tells me.

I nod, and we sit back, relax on the porch, wearing wigs.

AUGUST 3
Farmville

Lorraine is either dead to the world or in a coma or else a pharmaceutically induced sleep. Eventually, I'm able to rouse her. She is disoriented, disheveled. After she has a cigarette and a cup of Coca-Cola, I tell her, "Your mother came for Rudy about an hour ago. I said you were still asleep because we were up really late last night."

Lorraine's mother is keeping Rudy for the weekend. We make plans for what's left of the day: drive to Farmville to go to the Emporium, which is a big junk shop.

Lorraine gets dressed. Black silk toreador pants and a blouse with rhinestone spaghetti straps. Although my outfit—a Hawaiian-print sarong—is nowhere near as glamorous, I too go heavy on the makeup: eyeliner, shadows, vivid red lipstick, and circles of pink rouge on my cheeks because when you're wearing a wig, it's no time to be fresh-faced. Lorraine and I both wear sunglasses that are tinted dark green.

We decide that today we will not speak English. We will speak French. We studied French in school. We're not the least bit fluent, even though Lorraine claims she is because she has visited Paris more than once.

Halfway to Farmville, a bee flies in through the open car window. It scoots under my skirt and stings me on the thigh. I pull the stinger out and some sticky stuff attached to it, which is the bee's intestines. A bee disembowels itself just to cause you pain. For the remainder of the drive, I worry about anaphylactic shock, but I don't mention it because of how Lorraine can worry herself sick over nothing.

The digital clock atop First Virginia Bank reads 1:20/102°. The wigs fit like wool watch caps. Snug wool caps covered with synthetic hair. Synthetics don't breathe.

Before we go inside the Emporium, Lorraine reminds me, *"Parle le français, d'accord?"* Her French accent is entirely American.

We wander around the store, which is not air-conditioned and is very dusty. I pick up a blue vase, chipped at the base, and I call to Lorraine, *"Regarde. C'est jolie, n'est-ce pas?"*

But rather than commenting on the vase, Lorraine lets out a squeal. *"Allez ici! Maintenant!"* She is holding books. Four books. Hardcovers that look to be from the 1950s. They are mildewed. I read the titles. *Rendezvous at Dubrovnik, Love Needs No Passport, It Happened in Italy, The Berlin Affair.*

"Très, très bizarre," Lorraine says. She hasn't enough command of French to explain why this is odd, but she doesn't have to. It is bizarre indeed. In one way or another, these titles make reference to Lorraine's past, to her one great affair of the heart. Lorraine and Peter wore out bedsprings in New York, Frankfurt, Dubrovnik, Lake Como. When Lorraine lived in New York and worked in the travel business, Peter was one of her clients until he was transferred first home to Frankfurt, then to Dubrovnik, from there to Brazil, and finally home again. Initially, Peter's transfers didn't put much of a crimp in their affair. *Au contraire.* They jetted the world to be together, which was romantic. What did put a crimp in the affair was Peter's marrying his other girlfriend, the one he'd

had for seventeen years. She was cross-eyed and came from the same cutesy German village he did. Shortly after that, Lorraine went South and married Mac. A rendezvous in Dubrovnik seems like a long time ago. There is barely even a Dubrovnik anymore. It's been bombed into rubble.

We bring the vase and the four books to the cashier, who says, "That'll be three dollars and eleven cents." Lorraine and I stare at her blankly because *nous parlons pas d'anglais*.

"THREE DOLLARS AND E-LEV-EN CENTS," she raises her voice, as if that will make us understand.

The only place to eat in Farmville where they actually put silverware on the table is the Steer. Our waitress is as thin as a minute and deadpan. She offers no clues as to whether she's onto us—our wigs, our French—or not. Her lack of affect spooks me. Country music comes from the jukebox. We wear our dark glasses, and in our feeble pidgin French we talk of life: insanity and death. I wonder out loud if I am dying. Then, I admit to Lorraine, "You know what the hardest part of this ordeal is? Telling people what's wrong. It's very difficult for me to discuss the particulars."

Lorraine finds this baffling. She tells me that people in the South are always discussing the particulars of their ailments. Blood in stools, incontinence, pus-encrusted carbuncles, a surfeit of earwax. "We especially talk about such things at mealtime," she says, "when the family's all gathered together around the table. Nobody wants to miss out on hearing about mucus or tumors or funny-colored urine."

I think about this, the brashness of such talk in mixed company, and I conclude how I'm not ready for that.

The waitress brings the check, and I scratch where the bee stung me. Even through my green glasses and the dark of the restaurant, I see the red welt.

When we get back to Lorraine's house, we take off the wigs. Then, we feel bald. We sort of look bald too.

On her kitchen table, Lorraine wraps the books she bought in brown paper. She addresses the package to Peter. Although it's been a year or longer since she's had any word from him, and only a polite, perfunctory word at that, they mustn't ever forget. They must be reminded of what they lost: the Civil War, the World Wars, and each other.

After dinner, over coffee, Lorraine tells me the history of her house, how it used to belong to two sisters, Minna and Lucie. They had an invalid brother who died because they didn't feed him. Then Lorraine says, "Come live with me. People expect two crazy women to live in this house."

I ask if I can be Minna, the meaner of the sisters, and Lorraine says, "Seriously, don't die on me. If you die, I'll go insane."

And I remind her, "You already are insane."

AUGUST 4
Boydton

Wigless, we drive to get Mac at the prison, where he now lives in the bunkhouse. In addition to being Lorraine's estranged husband, Mac's a correctional officer and a drunk. He's a mess, but I like him anyway.

Mac is going to direct us to a flea market that's off a dirt road. Mac fancies American antiques and collects glass chickens. "So," Mac asks from the backseat, "what'd you all do yesterday?"

Lorraine says to me, "You tell him."

Mac appreciates the story about the wigs. "Goddamn, you all are crazy motherfuckers." Then he adds, "Oh, before I forget. The man who owns this flea market, he thinks I'm from Buckingham. So y'all don't say nothing about being from Chase City."

"Now why in the world would you do that?" Lorraine asks. "What possessed you to tell the man you're from Buckingham?"

"Same goddamn thing that possessed you all to dress up like French whores to go parading around Farmville."

"He makes a good point," I note.

"Goddamn right I make a goddamn point. Now pull on up to the E-Z store," Mac instructs. "I need to get me some beer."

Lorraine yells out the window after Mac to get us some Coca-Colas and two packs of generic cigarettes.

Carrying a brown paper bag against his chest, Mac is laughing all the while as he gets back in the car, passes up our sodas and smokes, and pops open a beer for himself. Then he tells us what's so funny. "Some goddamn niggers in there buying beer and pork skins and hot sauce and goddamn Ivory soap. They is headed to the river for a picnic and a bath. Pork skins. Hot sauce. Ivory soap. Niggers."

I can't get used to that, how people here say that word, say it blithely. It makes me want to cry. More than once, Lorraine has explained to me, "They know what they know. Black and white and that's that. They're ignorant."

On several occasions, while on visits down South, I've been asked what race I am. Total strangers coming up to me and asking, "What race are you?" And once, on line to buy cigarettes, a man said to me, "I bet you're from England. I can tell 'cause you ain't from around here."

"You are a damn fool," Lorraine said to the man. To me, she said, "See how they think? You're either from Virginia or England. Like there are no other places in the world."

The flea market is a junk-filled, dilapidated garage behind a hand-painted sign that reads EDDIE FLEAK MARKET.

I assume it should read EDDIE'S FLEA MARKET, but I could be wrong.

Lorraine buys two picture frames. I buy a cracked teacup, and Mac pockets an old postage stamp, which he shows us once we're back in the car. Eddie's wife had an envelope filled with them. Confederate stamps in all different colors. "She got hundreds of the motherfuckers," Mac says. "I bet they're worth a fortune."

We stop on the way home for Mac to relieve himself in the woods. Then, we stop again to get him more beer. "I'm warning you, Mac," Lorraine says. "If you get obnoxious, I'm pitching you out."

Mac is drunk when Lorraine's mother arrives to return Rudy. Before she leaves, Lorraine's mother tells me that Rudy had a loose bowel movement. "Nothing to worry over," she says. "Just not as firm as I'd like."

An hour later, during a fried-chicken dinner, Lorraine makes good on her word and throws Mac out of her house.

"Where will he go?" I ask. He can't go back to the bunkhouse drunk.

Lorraine shrugs. "He'll get himself a bottle of that Beauman's wine, drink it all up, and pass out in the toolshed or the woods somewhere. He's pitiful."

The welt from my bee sting has worsened. It's very red and raised up a half inch. It's also hot to the touch. I show it to Lorraine, and she suggests a poultice. I'm not exactly sure what that is, so I say, "No. No poultice." What I suggest we do instead is put on our wigs, sit on the porch, and listen to the crickets.

"What if the neighbors see me?" Lorraine worries. "What if Mrs. Nestel peeks out and sees us through her window? People don't sit on the porch in the dark. It's not done here. After dinner, yes, but once the sun goes down, you go inside."

In the night, on the porch, we settle in. Lorraine watches for neighbors spying. I watch the glow of a firefly blink on and off like Tinker Bell, and Rudy, pointing at airplane lights gliding through the black sky, says, "Star."

AUGUST 5
Boydton (again)

Like we've got on berets or tams, we wear our wigs at a jaunty angle. A wig askew looks demented. As we drink our coffee and decide we might like to stroll around town disguised as

Minna and Lucie, Mac comes in. He's looking for his wallet. He overhears Lorraine tell me, "It's his wallet or his watch. He gets drunk as a fish and can never find one or the other."

"Yeah, well, you all look like damn fools in them wigs," Mac retorts. "You don't even got them on right."

Mac finds his wallet behind the couch and then sits with us. The conversation turns to his grandfather who fried squirrels to eat. "Heads and all. Yep, scooped out the brains and ate them." Mac demonstrates how to eat squirrel brains by dipping a crooked index finger like Jack Horner with a plum and popping it into his mouth. From there we move on to the subject of cow flops, which Mac claims are an aphrodisiac. "The smell makes my dick hard. Oh, yeah, fucking on some old barn floor." Mac lets go with a hoot. Lorraine is on the kitchen floor, curled up in the fetal position.

Figuring Mac knows a thing or two about bee stings, I show him mine.

"Yep," he says. "That's a bee sting all right. You get the sticker out?" Then, he makes a lewd comment about stickers and my thigh.

Lorraine sits up and asks if we should take me to the hospital. In unison Mac and I say, "No."

The real reason Mac is here has nothing to do with his lost wallet. He has cooked up a scheme to get the rest of the Confederate stamps from Eddie Fleak Market. He needs Lorraine and me to abet and Rudy as a decoy. "With the boy," Mac says, "we'll look like nice family people."

Along the way, Mac gets drunk. Lorraine complains that

her wig itches, but she refuses to take it off. My bee sting throbs. Rudy squalls for his ba-ba, which he left at home. Still, I'm happy to be winding along this country road with Lorraine, wearing our wigs, planning a heist.

The plan is to prepare to buy a bunch of junk and then ask about the stamps as if they were an afterthought, the way teenagers buy condoms or glue to sniff. If Eddie and his wife think they might lose the whole sale, maybe they'll throw in the stamps at a bargain price.

Mac picks out a highboy that's home to a family of spiders and two warped LPs, Hank Williams. To this he adds a glass statue of a dog, its tail snapped off. Then he cracks under pressure and pays thirty-five dollars up front for this crap. However, when he recovers well enough to ask, "Hey, you still got them stamps? For the boy here," gesturing at Rudy, Eddie seems willing to sell them for a song. His wife, on the other hand, is not so willing.

Those Confederate stamps came off the love letters her grandfather's Uncle Eli wrote during the Civil War to his fiancée, who was also his second cousin. And although Carrie Oaks went and married some other man, the stamps are family history. Also, Eddie's wife isn't sure what they're worth, and while she tries to calculate that kind of value, Lorraine does her part by throwing a fit. "Stamps," she shouts. "Why not buy up the whole goddamn store, Mac? Stamps," she snorts at the foolishness of such a purchase. "Bunch of worn-out stamps for a child not even two years old."

Eddie's wife takes the bait. She sells the envelope filled

with Confederate stamps—stamps that her ancestor sent along with hope and desire—for ten bucks.

We haven't pulled out of the driveway before Mac whoops and hollers, "We're rich! These stamps got to be worth a million dollars. Five million!" Mac wants to spend the money on a new truck, maybe a boat, and a gas grill.

"Shut up, Mac." Lorraine's patience is waning.

As soon as he gets in the house, Mac passes out in front of the television. Lorraine, Rudy, and I have dinner. Chicken in barbecue sauce that's been simmering in the Crock-Pot since yesterday.

After Rudy has his bath and is tucked into bed, Lorraine joins me on the porch. Mac wakes and comes out too. Lorraine refuses to look at him, but she tells him it's my last night here. "We want to be alone without you pestering us."

"You want me to leave?" Mac asks. "Is that it?"

"Yes," Lorraine says.

"Well, why didn't you just say so?"

"I did just say so," Lorraine speaks through clenched teeth.

But Mac doesn't want to leave. Other than to the prison bunkhouse, he's got nowhere to go. He turns, goes back inside the house, and watches the race cars on TV.

"Oh, Minna," Lorraine sighs.

"Oh Lucie," I sigh too.

"I don't want you to leave," Lorraine whispers.

If I stayed, if I moved into that bedroom where the sisters let their brother starve to death, then every night Lorraine and I could put on our wigs and sit out here in the dark.

People expect two crazy women to live in this house. On Halloween, the neighborhood children would dare each other to come up our porch steps.

But I can't stay on in a place where no one can figure out who and what I am, except that I might be an alien from England. I have no claim to this red soil and no urge to grab a fistful of it and hold it to my breast.

"You're going back tomorrow, aren't you?" Lorraine asks, and I tell her yes.

AUGUST 6
En Route: Richmond to New York

I had planned to wear my wig on the train, but I decide that it would be too much like wearing a party hat long after the guests have gone home. The wig goes in my suitcase with the chipped vase, the cracked teacup, and my Hawaiian-print sarong.

It's a two-hour drive to Richmond. Plus we need to allow an extra hour because Richmond is a city Lorraine is unable to navigate. "People vanish in Richmond," she says. "Also, we'll want to stop and eat."

Before we leave Chase City, we go to the post office to mail the package of books to Peter. "How do you think he'll respond?" Lorraine asks me, and I say, "He'll feel sad and ashamed of himself."

"Good," Lorraine says.

Rudy, such a sweet boy, falls asleep in his car seat, and

Lorraine asks me, "Should I feel bad because I didn't show you the sights of Virginia?"

I assure her I have no need to see the place where Lee surrendered.

Then Lorraine expresses fear that once I'm gone she might very well crawl back into bed and stay there, again neglecting to keep herself clean.

"So you forget to shower now and then," I make light. "Big deal. Spritz some perfume under your arms. No one will know the difference."

"Don't die on me," Lorraine whispers. "Promise me."

"I promise I won't die on you," I say, as if I could really promise such a thing.

Rudy wakes when we pull in at the Shoney's next to the train station. We take a booth, and Lorraine tells the waitress we're in a hurry. "We have a train to catch." She makes it sound as if she and Rudy were coming with me. I tousle Rudy's blond hair.

Rudy gets more ice cream on his face than in his mouth, and Lorraine moves meat loaf around and around on her plate. I pick at the iceberg lettuce in my salad.

At the train station, Lorraine pulls up at a No Parking sign. She gets my suitcase from the backseat while I kiss Rudy good-bye on the tip of his nose. He giggles and says, "Eyes."

To Rudy, all facial features are *eyes*, just as all animals are *doggie*, and anything not room temperature—even ice cream—is *hot*. It's a good worldview.

I board the train and sit in a No Smoking car. I have to

quit cigarettes by the time I get home to my husband, and to the doctors, all of whom I swore to that I do not smoke cigarettes. I lean into my seat, open my book, and doze off.

When I wake, the train is pulling into Baltimore Station. Outside it is dark, night. The beam from the overhead light casts a melancholy glow. I make my way to the club car and buy a box of peanut M&M's and a Coke. Dinner. My last meal until the day after tomorrow, after the doctors are done with yet another round of tests.

My summer plans never included this, this getting sick, vials of my blood drawn by efficient technicians, pictures snapped of my inner organs, poked and prodded by doctors. I try not to think about any of it, and instead I think about what compels Lorraine to live in a place that is bent on breaking her heart. How did her long-dead ancestors reach up from their graves to pull her back, to hold her to this land where her family tree has thick and tangled roots deep beneath the red soil?

And I wonder what I will do with my wig once I'm home in New York. Probably I'll put it away in a keepsake box, as if it were something like stamps from love letters written long ago.

I

In August of the election year, the Kennedy/Nixon election year, we were most often found sitting on the curb discussing things. We were too little for summer camp or to go off the block even, so we'd park ourselves on the curb in front of our houses where our mothers could keep an eye on us.

Children ought to be kept busy or else they become horrid. Or maybe that had nothing to do with it. Regardless, we were fabulous squabblers, squawking birds pecking at each other's head. Our aim was nothing less than to wound, to draw tears. With this desired end, we would then respond with the sort of innocence often attributed to children by those who know nothing about them. "We were only fooling," we'd say. "We didn't mean to make anyone cry."

This bickering on the curb rarely failed to peak with an index finger—one so small you could hardly make out the nail—pointing at she who had displeased us and ordering her to "Get off my property." Such a fall from grace was generally due to some infraction—cheating at jacks, cutting one, sneezing without a tissue—of our breathtakingly rigid code of behavior.

"It's not your property," Carine Rainer would say. "It's your father's property. Only your father can kick me off." Carine Rainer was an immaculate child who once had some kind of seizure when she got a grass stain on a lemon-colored skirt.

My opinion was that the curb belonged to the government, and no one but a policeman had authority over it. However, dare one blade of grass get between the offending party and the curb at my house, then you were without a doubt on my property and subject to trespass violations.

Buffy Donovan maintained that the curb, like all things in the world and everywhere else too, belonged to God. Buffy Donovan taught us to recite the Hail Mary as a necessary part of a game called Confession. Another game Buffy dreamed up was called Nun, the rules to which were fuzzy. It began with Buffy assigning us boy names—Sister Thomas Edmund or Xavier Francis. We were all Sister Something or Other except when Jeffrey Quinn was around. Buffy dubbed him the Bishop. However, once the name business was done with, Nun quickly fizzled out because not even Buffy Donovan knew for sure what it was nuns did.

My mother called the Donovans "Lace-Curtain Irish,"

which seemed fitting to me, as Buffy was creamy-skinned and had light blue eyes and looked as if she'd billow in a cross-breeze.

The Kennedys were also Lace-Curtain Irish, only my mother sounded tolerant when referring to them, as if the Kennedys couldn't help it but the Donovans could.

My parents, it turned out, were the only Kennedy supporters on our block. They weren't fanatics. They didn't deck themselves out with JFK buttons or wear JFK straw hats or JFK sashes the way that college girl who came to our house with pamphlets did. But they were going to vote for him. They told me so, although my father's reasons went over my head, fat words that drifted lazily upward, like the Goodyear blimp, and out of my grasp. When I asked my mother why she was going to vote for John F. Kennedy, she carried on, for too long, about how handsome he was.

I fully expected the Donovans to vote for Kennedy because of the Lace-Curtain Irish connection. Such clannishness weighed heavily in our quest for common ground. We were quite big on joining forces, banding together before breaking apart only to scramble to regroup with all the frenzy of a round of musical chairs. We formed clubs, clubs for those of us whose phone numbers began with 335, clubs for people who lived in white houses. We had a Methodist Club and a Blue Bicycle Club. We stopped at nothing to make certain we belonged.

And what better way to sure up your own inclusion than to exclude another? To guarantee you were in, all you had to do was boot Carine Rainer out. That was why we had a club for people with brown hair. We elected a president, a VP, and set dues—which never got collected—at ten cents. A surefire way to ostracize Priss Crawford was to start a club for those of us wearing white shirts. Priss Crawford wasn't allowed to wear white shirts because her mother said you could see through them in direct sunlight. To be different was the worst thing that could happen.

Yet, Lace-Curtain Irish proved not enough to align the Donovans with John F. Kennedy. Buffy Donovan told us her mother said John Kennedy was a bad Catholic and was going to go straight to hell. Hell was a place Buffy had previously told us all about, filling us in on the details of flames and pits filled with hot coals, and devils with horns and tails, and torture chambers with thumbscrews. Buffy told us all about eternity, stuff my mother said I wasn't to pay any attention to. "Catholic mumbo jumbo," my mother said.

According to Buffy Donovan's father, John F. Kennedy was a Communist who was going to give the country away to the niggers and the Jews.

It was very unsettling to discover I was the only one out on the curb who was for Kennedy. In part, I feared that the others would, at any moment, start a Nixon club. But I was also impressed with my own opinions, such as they were my own. Impressed enough to lie for them. "Do you know," I asked my circle of tiny friends, "what Nixon said in his last speech?"

As I was the only one of us who could read and write with any proficiency, they had little choice but to give me their attention. Carine could write her name, only her *E* at the end faced in, which was the wrong way to make an *E*, so it didn't count.

"Nixon said,"—I lowered my voice to draw them in closer—"that if he gets elected, the first thing he's going to do is round up all dogs. All dogs," I repeated, "and gas them."

The enormity of this proposal was enough to stun even me, who, but a moment ago, knew it to be a whopping lie. However, once said aloud, it took on the dimensions of real possibility.

The responsibility of such gruesome knowledge forced our mouths to hang open, but no words could come out. We were wishing we'd never heard such a thing. We had no idea that presidents did not have the same power of decree as the kings and queens of fairy tales. If Nixon wanted to do this— he could.

Most of us had dogs. Mine was a sweet-tempered terrier named Sandy, who, two years later, had a litter of four puppies. This resulted in the Donovans not speaking to us for several months because my mother let Buffy watch the puppies get born. Sandy was also the name of Orphan Annie's dog, which was where we got the name from.

The Donovans resumed neighborly relations with us when my grandmother died. Mrs. Donovan came to our house and told me I should be happy that my grandmother was now with God. Mrs. Donovan said God took my grandmother because she was such a good person, He wanted her in heaven with Him. As far as I was concerned, that was a pretty selfish thing for God to do.

After Mrs. Donovan left, my mother told me to never

mind what she'd said. "It's the way Irish Catholics comfort," my mother told me. "They believe so much in a literal heaven that when one of their own dies, they throw a party to celebrate the dead person's union with God. A real party," my mother explained, "with cocktails and hors d'oeuvres and dancing."

It sounded to me like Irish Catholics were screwy in the head.

"Maybe so," my mother said, "but that's the kind of opinion you have to keep to yourself."

Two of the girl dogs on our block were named Lady, directly from the Disney movie, although no one named the boy dogs Tramp. Boy dogs were called Prince or Blackie. The Quinns had a collie named Lassie. The thought of our dogs being taken from us was ghastly enough, I'd assumed, to change everyone's vote.

Except Priss Crawford said I was a liar, that Nixon wasn't going to gas all dogs. "Just the dogs of the people who voted for Kennedy," Priss said. Priss Crawford, over the years, grew very fat and did something so scandalous with a gang of boys that the Crawfords moved away without even selling their house first. This was around the time my friend Amy and I sat in her room trying to define the verb *to finger*.

As my friends were now able to keep their dogs, along with their parents' politics, intact, this subject was dropped. Carine Rainer wanted to play Barbie.

Besides dressing and undressing the dolls, playing Barbie involved nothing other than the challenge to steal each other's Barbie shoes. Barbie shoes, owing to their size, had a way of getting lost almost instantly. So whether in her nurse's uniform or gold lamé evening gown with fur wrap, Barbie was often barefoot. We loathed incompleteness to such a degree that we thought nothing of stealing to prevent it. If you happened to have a pair of shoes for your Barbie, it behooved you to keep your eyes on them. Mostly though, we stole Barbie shoes from Ilene Harrison, because she had a clubfoot.

I did not want to play Barbie. Barbie was stupid, and I told my friends as much. Plus I told them I hated their guts. I went home and found my mother sunning herself in the backyard. I sat at the foot of her chaise longue and asked her whom Bob the Good Humor man was going to vote for. Bob was popular on my block because he tweaked our noses, knew our names, and always had chocolate-covered cones on hand. To have the Good Humor man on my side would have to count for something.

II

The Bay of Pigs was a pond in Florida where pigs swam. The pigs were not smelly, hog-size animals with tufts of coarse hair, but pink, cuddly creatures looking like Wilbur from *Charlotte's Web*. These pigs—and there were hundreds of them splashing, dunking, diving—frolicked in the pond the same way we did in the summer months in our swimming pools.

Nearly every family on our block had a swimming pool, so you could swim laps unimpeded, except no one wanted to. Pools were fun only when you piled in as many kids as would fit. Before inviting all the kids into your pool, you had to get your mother's permission. Mothers had to be there to make sure no one drowned. Also, mothers had to serve Hawaiian Punch and watermelon while we dried off because it was expected. Pretty much, we invaded pools by rotation. Mothers took turns giving the okay.

The Crawfords' turn didn't come up as often as some. The first time we were allowed in their pool was well into July. Mrs. Crawford watched us from the kitchen window. Priss explained she did not watch us from a poolside chair the way the other mothers did because her mother burned easily if she sat out in the sun.

Having been dunked by Jeffrey Quinn, I surfaced to witness the Crawfords' back door swing open. Mrs. Crawford bustled out and across the lawn, which was already squooshy from our splashing. She looked like a bull I'd seen in a cartoon as she charged toward the pool. In one swoop, Mrs. Crawford plucked Rachel Rosenberg from the water and deposited her on the grass. "There's not enough room for you, dear," Mrs. Crawford said to Rachel Rosenberg. "You go on home and swim in your own pool."

The Rosenbergs' pool was built-in and much better than the Crawfords' pool, which was only three feet deep and made of corrugated tin lined with a rubber sheet. I stood at the edge and watched Rachel Rosenberg slip into her flip-flops and gather up her towel. I was hoping she'd invite me to go along with her. Her pool even had a diving board.

When the summer was over, Buffy Donovan didn't go to the same school as the rest of us. She went to a Catholic school and wore a uniform, a plaid jumper over a white blouse, a blue blazer with an insignia on the pocket, white knee socks, and brown oxford shoes that were extremely ugly. The name of Buffy's school was Our Lady of Perpetual Devotion.

At P.S. 36, we didn't wear uniforms. We wore whatever our mothers dressed us in. This was risky because your mother could dress you in something queer, and then you wouldn't have any friends.

I wanted a uniform like Buffy's, especially the blue blazer with the insignia. I wanted to go to the Catholic school, but my mother said, "No way in hell."

Buffy Donovan said the public school was a Jew school. Priss Crawford said it was not.

While we were taught the Pledge of Allegiance, Buffy Donovan was learning to recite something called Baltimore Catechism.

I asked my mother if Caroline Kennedy and John John would be going to Catholic school like Buffy Donovan. My mother said that wasn't likely. "It wouldn't be good politics," she said, which I took to mean that Buffy Donovan was not a good American.

On Wednesday mornings, the music teacher came to our class. She had fat legs. With the aid of a pitch pipe, she led us in song, "The Star-Spangled Banner" and "America, the Beautiful."

At our school, we had three sorts of drills. My favorite was the fire drill because we got to go outside, even though we did have to stand in line and were forbidden to talk. The other drills were bomb drills. One had us file into the hall and face the lockers with our hands clamped around the backs of our necks. The other bomb drill sent us under our desks, which were supposed to double as fall-out shelters.

The art teacher came on Friday afternoons from one-thirty to two-thirty. Her name was Miss Gilbert, and she was pretty. She wore a paint-stained smock with big pockets, and she let us draw whatever we wanted to.

I drew the Bay of Pigs. Pigs were easy to draw. You made them like snowmen who'd fallen on their sides. After adding triangular ears and corkscrew tails, they got colored pink.

Even though I knew for certain that the Bay of Pigs was a pond with reeds growing up from the bottom, I drew it as Rachel Rosenberg's swimming pool, rectangle-shaped and blue and clear. I drew one pig, toe-dancing, on the diving board.

III

Mostly we got watched because our mothers were having babies. Getting watched was not the same thing as being baby-sat. Baby-sitters were teenagers who took care of us when our parents went out at night. My regular baby-sitter was Billy. I loved him because he knew many things about the Kennedys. When I asked him who baby-sat for Caroline and John John when the president and Jackie went to the movies, he told me, "Secret Service." To show me who Secret Service was, Billy put a transistor radio plug in his ear and made his face go stern. The object of the game, he said, was to get Secret Service to laugh.

On nights when Billy wasn't available, Gail baby-sat me. Gail was ignorant of the goings-on at the White House. "How should I know?" she said when I asked if Caroline wore Dr. Denton's feetie pajamas like I did.

Gail also tended to put me to bed at eight o'clock, whereas Billy didn't have any rules and let me watch *Twilight Zone* in the dark.

Once I overheard Mrs. Crawford say to Mrs. Donovan how it was shameful that my mother allowed a teenage boy to baby-sit me. She said it was asking for trouble, and Mrs. Donovan agreed.

Getting watched was never at night, but during the day when your mother went to the doctor for baby checkups, and a neighbor looked after you. Our mothers dropped babies fairly regularly—that is, once or twice a year a baby was born to a family on our block—up until the end of 1963, and then they pretty much stopped.

Jackie Kennedy was having a baby at the same time my mother was and Mrs. Rainer too. Everything Jackie Kennedy did was enormously popular. Despite that a lot of mothers continued to insist they didn't like her, they all took to wearing pillbox hats and straight skirts with matching box jackets. At the A&P they looked like a packet of multicolored, eraser-topped pencils pushing shopping carts. A large number of our mothers took to wearing their hair in the same style as Jackie. My mother said Jackie Kennedy was a lady.

When Mrs. Rainer watched me on Tuesdays, my mother's day with Dr. Gottlieb, Carine and I would sit in her family room and try hard not to make a mess. No one ever believed me, but once I did see Mrs. Rainer take Carine by the neck and bang her head against the bathroom wall because Carine spilled soda on the carpet.

On Thursdays, Mrs. Rainer's day with the doctor, Carine and I played in my bedroom, which was identical (I had my father's word on this) to Caroline Kennedy's bedroom in the White House. Caroline and I both had white canopy beds with pink organdy spreads and throw pillows. Because it was my bedroom, I got to be Caroline. Jackie Kennedy was played by Carine. My teddy bear stood in for John John. We didn't need a President Kennedy. He was a father, and we didn't consider fathers much. Mothers we understood, and Jackie Kennedy was a mother who was having a baby too. And Caroline Kennedy, she was the same as us, only she was sort of a princess. I saw a picture in *Life* magazine of Caroline Kennedy with her pony.

Playing the First Family, Carine and I planned Caroline's birthday party. We made a list of which movie stars and kids on our block to invite. We decided on a menu of animal crackers and Yoo-Hoo. We'd seen a photograph, also in *Life* magazine, of Caroline's real birthday party, of Caroline cutting into a cake, John and Jackie standing over her. But in later years, whenever I tried to bring that picture to mind, I kept seeing, instead, a still of John Kennedy's birthday party, the one where Marilyn Monroe sang "Happy Birthday, Mr. President," in her itty-bitty voice.

Jackie Kennedy's baby died two weeks before my brother Michael was born. I didn't want a brother. I wanted a sister. The Kennedys named their baby Patrick, but still he didn't live. There was a televised mass said for baby Patrick Kennedy. Jackie was there all in black, a veil covering her face. Someone, a man, was holding her at the elbow. Or maybe that was another televised mass said over another Kennedy death.

When Jackie's baby died, my mother sat me down and explained that while baby Patrick Kennedy did not live, there was no reason to worry about her baby. "Our baby is going to be just fine," my mother said. I already knew this. The sort of tragedy that had befallen the Kennedys was too royal to happen at our house. Still, if I had to get a brother, I'd have preferred one who died on us.

The day my parents brought Michael home from the hospital, along with a nursemaid named Darcy, who was a Negro, I got a Serving Suzy Electric Oven Baking Set. With heat generated from a bulb, I could bake little cakes the size of cookies in it.

With a sister, but not one named Caroline even though

she said that was the name her mother had decided on, Carine Rainer got a Chatty Cathy doll.

Buffy Donovan said it was a lucky thing that the Kennedys had baby Patrick baptized before he died. Baptism was the way into heaven. Otherwise, Buffy told us, baby Patrick would've gone to a place called purgatory, which, from the way she described it, sounded nice enough to me. Only Buffy said purgatory was awful because you weren't with God. Buffy had us kneel and say a prayer for baby Patrick Kennedy's soul. Buffy had also been trying to get us to learn a new prayer, one that had a line that went, "If I should die before I wake." That line gave me the creeps, and I told Buffy so. I refused to say it because it was like making an ugly face that could stick.

In September 1962, Mrs. Montoban, who lived behind us and already had four children, had one more. My mother said having five children was vulgar. The Montobans named their newest one John Glenn after the astronaut. John Glenn Montoban had ears that stuck way out.

IV

Negroes were moving into our neighborhood. Not onto our block but onto Westwind Road, which was two streets away if you went up Allen and took a right at Willow. At first, their house wasn't a house at all. It was a plot of land. The Negroes were going to build their house from scratch.

The father of the Negro family was an architect, and the mother was a librarian. They had two children, a boy who was seven and a girl who was four. Their name was Wilson. We had all this information before their house even went up for good. Usually we knew next to nothing about a new family until after they moved in and the Welcome Wagon paid a visit. The Welcome Wagon was our mothers, armed with cakes and pies and casseroles, trooping over to welcome the new family to the neighborhood. They gave them the cakes and stuff, plus a list of stores and baby-sitters, and the phone number of Dr. Strictman, who was the pediatrician.

Whenever my mother returned from a Welcome Wagon outing, she would tell me how many children the new family had, what the father did for a living, and how their house was decorated.

Our house was decorated Early American. Most of the other houses on our block were done in what my mother called Contemporary. I wished we had Contemporary because that's what the majority had. The inherent right of the majority to rule was the bedrock of democracy. In all matters, I wished to be of that class. Whatever the majority had, or wanted, was right and best, and so Contemporary furniture had to be nicer than Early American. Except my mother didn't see it that way. She said our neighbors shopped at Sears for their furniture. She said this as if there were something wrong with Sears furniture, which there couldn't have been because it was the majority.

Mr. Donovan was furious that Negroes were moving into

our neighborhood. He blamed it on President Kennedy and came over to our house to talk to my parents about the problem. My father expressed concern over something called property values, which was somehow related to the Negroes.

I found it curious that we knew so much about the Wilsons before their house was anything but a bunch of cinder blocks. To see if I could find out anything else, I rode over there on my bicycle. I was hoping the Wilsons would decorate Early American.

Before the Wilsons' house went up and stayed up, it was burned down three times. My mother said that was terrible, especially sad because these Negroes were of good quality. "They're educated people," my mother said. "Still, you can't really blame people for being concerned about their investments."

The only other Negroes I'd ever met were Darcy, who changed my baby brother's diapers, and Helen, who came to our house every Saturday to help my mother with the heavy cleaning. Heavy cleaning was waxing floors, washing windows, polishing silver. Helen was tall and skinny and laughed like a madwoman. I liked Helen better than Clara, the other Negro woman I knew. Clara did the Rainers' ironing, and she yelled and told on us when she found me ironing the curls out of Carine's hair. Clara didn't iron at our house because my mother sent my father's shirts to Chinese people. I never saw a Negro man in person until the Wilsons moved in.

Buffy Donovan called Charlene Wilson, who was not as cute as I'd imagined she would be, "nigger" to her face. Also

Buffy said, "Get off my block, you ugly colored girl." I had imagined Charlene Wilson would wear her hair in a hundred little braids tied with brightly colored ribbons, but she didn't.

President Kennedy wanted to make things better for Negroes in the South. We didn't live in the South.

My mother said the whole neighborhood held its breath when the Wilson house went up for sale. But in the end, everyone relaxed because the Wilsons sold their house to a white family with two darling girls and a baby on the way. Once again, we learned of this before these white people moved in. My mother said the Wilsons were moving away because they didn't like Westwind Road. All totaled, they didn't live seven months in the house they built.

Everyone, it seems, remembers exactly where they were and what they were doing when President Kennedy got shot. I was in the second grade reciting the multiplication tables—6 X 4 = 24, 6 X 5 = 30—when the principal's voice broke over the PA system. Stephanie Obertz, who sat next to me, began to cry but said it didn't have anything to do with John F. Kennedy getting shot. Stephanie Obertz said she had a stomachache.

After that, it was as if guns went off in succession; three fatal bullets from one clip.

The Wilsons moved away the same day President Kennedy was buried. Those two events didn't have anything to do with each other, although for many, many years I thought they did.

courtship

This morning, a few hours before checking into the hospital, my mother went and had her hair done. She got a manicure and a pedicure too. As if going in for heart surgery were the same as going to a dinner dance, she got all dolled up. Refusing a puke-green hospital gown, my mother wears a cream-colored silk nightie. She has on lipstick, mascara, eyeshadow, and gold earrings. Here, lounging in a hospital bed, she looks gorgeous. But she always looks gorgeous. My mother is a dish.

It is my father who looks sick. He is pale, withdrawn, and says nothing while my mother—the belle of the intensive care unit—chats and laughs and flirts with the doctors and nurses who are in and out taking blood pressure, temperature, case histories. Charts in hand, they ask my mother if she's had any other surgical procedures. Which childhood diseases has she been exposed to? Is she allergic to any medication? None of their questions will reveal anything about the state of my mother's heart. For that, they should talk to my father.

The orderlies, two handsome young men with strong arms, come to wheel my mother off to surgery. I feel like I'm watching a scene from *General Hospital*. A soap-opera star and a pair of extras. Only my father looks like a real person. I turn to him and say, "Go home. Get some sleep." The operation is scheduled to be long, eight hours, and intricate. There's no reason to wait here. But my father shakes his head. He does not say so, but I'm sure it's that he can't imagine sleeping in their bed without her.

My parents met after the war. Because my mother fudges all dates to keep her age a mystery, I don't know the exact year, but probably it was '48 or '49. I do know my mother was only seventeen. My father was older, twenty-two, and a man of the world. He'd been to Paris, but came home to the Bronx where he went to a party hosted by a funny-looking girl named Esther. Esther wore blue-rimmed eyeglasses and bobby socks and was nothing at all like the French women, who wore perfume and nylons despite shortages and rations.

My mother attended the High School of Art and Design with Esther, of whom she was not overly fond because Esther had a big mouth and no style. Still, she went to Esther's party because she had nothing else to do. Her steady boyfriend, who played the saxophone, and also, according to Esther, smoked marijuana, was working a wedding. My mother was not one to stay home alone on a Saturday night.

Right away she spotted him, my father. He was handsome. Movie-star handsome, she told me. Tall, broad-shouldered, dark-eyed, wavy black hair, and a smile that turned her insides to goop. But when he approached her, my mother blushed like the schoolgirl she was, like the young Judy Garland singing her love letter to Clark Gable. Desperate to appear older and sophisticated (after all, she was from Manhattan and not the Bronx like the other girls there), my mother said to my father what she thought a cosmopolitan woman would say under such circumstances: *I'm sorry I can't talk to you. I'm waiting for my husband.*

At the end of the night, not willing to leave without her, my father went back over to my mother and said, "Are you still waiting for your husband?"

Looking my father dead in the eye, my mother said, "What husband?" In those two or three hours of sitting on the couch at a party in the Bronx, fuming at her own ineptness, my mother had become a woman.

They went walking through Bronx Park, something you could actually do back then, and there by a tree, as if perched on the tip of the crescent moon, they kissed. When the kiss ended, my father said, "Marry me," and my mother said, "Yes."

When I was still a child but definitely on my way to contemplating boys, a preteen, I considered the story of my parents' engagement to be an unbearably romantic escapade. Often I mused that someday a handsome man would propose marriage to me after having just met me too. "Oh," my mother said. "I wouldn't be happy about that. It was a foolish thing for me to have done. It was only blind luck that it turned out so right."

But my mother was mistaken. It wasn't blind luck. It was the kind of love that only seems like blind luck. She also misunderstood what it was I wanted. I wanted only the proposal. Not the rest of it. I wanted to be asked, and I wanted to refuse. I never imagined saying yes the way my mother did.

Not long after that, but long enough for me to have learned a few more things, I cornered my mother and asked, "Were you a virgin when you got married?"

My mother said she was, but she admitted, "Only because I was so young, and it all happened so fast. If we'd waited longer to be married . . ." Her words trailed off, but even at an age when I'd not yet been properly kissed, I realized there were things that could be delayed for only so long and then not at all.

Occasionally a practical woman, my mother did not advise me to wait until my wedding night. She said to wait only until I found someone I loved, but I rarely took my mother's advice on any subject.

The reason my parents waited three months to be married from the night they walked in Bronx Park was because my mother wanted a whoop-de-do of a wedding. Her father consented to her wishes, but he was opposed to them. He and my grandmother had eloped, taking the train one night to Baltimore, and while he didn't exactly suggest his daughter do that, he did suggest my parents marry in a judge's chamber followed by a cocktail party. "Keep it simple," he said, but my mother was bent on the whole shebang. She wore a gown with a six-foot train. She had five bridesmaids, and Esther was her maid of honor.

My mother kept her wedding gown in a box in the attic. I used to steal up there to look at it, to stroke the satin, finger the lace, and wonder about my own future, which seemed distant and not at all clear.

One day my mother came downstairs carrying her wedding gown to put in the garbage. "I was saving it for you, but it's a mess," she said. "All wrinkled and water-stained." My mother can be a sentimental woman except when it comes to useless clutter. But before throwing her gown away, she cut off the lace collar and cuffs and gave them to me. Later, I sewed the collar and cuffs of my mother's wedding gown onto a denim jacket.

Her parents, my grandparents, were apparently not concerned by the speed with which lightning struck their daughter and future son-in-law. They thought it sweet. To meet my father, to get to know him, they planned a family picnic. My grandparents on my mother's side were already third-generation Americans. My grandfather was an avid fly fisherman, and my grandmother, having been raised in a home and time when there was a lot of money, learned to play the piano but not how to cook.

Grandmothers, in general, are often found bent over hot ovens baking chocolate chip or poppy seed cookies. Most grandmothers implore an invariably too skinny grandchild to eat, eat, eat, but when I visited this grandmother she offered only, "Would you like a banana?"

They died young, my maternal grandparents. My grandfather went first. His heart gave out. Shortly after that, my grandmother simply died.

My mother's people were not of strong constitution, and I wonder if my father is thinking about that now. Is he worried that she's inherited her father's faulty heart or her mother's heart, one that was unable to mend?

Or is my father lost in time? Has he returned to that picnic by a stream, my grandfather thigh-deep in the water casting for bass, my mother and grandmother sitting under a shade tree, their dresses fanned out around them? When it was time to eat, my grandmother opened a wicker basket and passed around the sandwiches she'd made.

To this day, my father will laugh and say, "Never in my life had I seen such a sandwich. Two slices of packaged white bread—I didn't even know there was such a thing as packaged white bread—and a thin slice of cheese in the middle." My father always brings his thumb and index finger within a millimeter of each other to illustrate just how thin that slice of cheese was. "That was it. Not even a piece of tomato or some mustard." While my father held this waferlike sandwich, my grandfather said to his wife, "Anne, you fussed," which my father thought was a family joke until he saw my grandmother lower her eyes at the praise and say, "Well, it is a special occasion." Then my father wondered if, by marrying into this family, he'd go hungry.

My father did not go hungry, but nor did he ever really eat

well again. Flawed hearts and culinary ineptitude appear to be genetic dispositions. But as with our varieties of heart ailments, the manifestations of our poor cooking skills mutate from generation to generation. Like my grandmother, I don't often find myself in the kitchen. However, when I do make something to eat, I lay the food out pleasingly on the plate. I'm handy with a garnish—a sprig of parsley, a radish rosette. I have lovely presentation, but the food I prepare is bland, no tastier than a boiled egg. Conversely, my mother never quit trying to whip up a good meal despite the slop she wound up with—charred-to-ash steaks, gloppy casseroles, flat omelettes, and how does a person burn asparagus?

For her first dinner party as a young newlywed living in a garden apartment in Queens, my mother made soggy spaghetti with meatballs that were raw in the center. Although her meals are as dreadful to look at as they are to eat, my mother sets a beautiful table—linen cloth and napkins, crystal goblets, fresh-cut flowers, bone-china plates. When her dinner guests left—no doubt for a pizza—my mother recalled how she'd seen other women, older, experienced women, shake their linen tablecloths out the window to rid them of all crumbs. Ever so desirous to play the part of the competent wife, my mother shook her tablecloth out the window too. Only she didn't clear it off first, and along with the crumbs, she tossed out the dessert plates, the coffee cups and saucers, the teaspoons, the sugar, the cream, and a vase filled with calla lilies. She and my father giggled as they went down the flight of stairs, and under the stars they picked up whatever hadn't broken in the fall.

Some other man might've grown annoyed by the daily fetid surprise on a dish my mother brought forth. But some other man didn't adore his wife like my father adores my mother, in that way where everything she does is priceless even when it isn't.

Not everyone adores my mother though. My father's sister Ruth, for example, never liked her. Ruth, burdened with two kids and a no-good husband, relied on my father to help out. Every Wednesday my father left money for his sister under the teapot. Fearful that this cash flow would dry up once my father married and had a family of his own, Ruth called my mother and said, "I'm glad he's marrying you. Not that he'll ever really get over that woman in Europe, the baroness, his great love, but at least he'll have a wife." Should that not have been enough to cause my mother to break off the engagement, Ruth added, "You do know about the insanity in our family, don't you?"

"Oh, yes," my mother said. "I know all about you."

My mother also knew what there was to know about the baroness, that she was part of a time and place before my parents met, and that the time before my parents met was a time that was over. In my father's life, all that remained of the baroness was a picture of her he kept with his other war mementos—his Purple Heart, his sergeant stripes, his discharge papers. The baroness had a Veronica Lake hairdo, dipping over one eye. She looked like the kind of woman who was likely to have a husky voice.

Of age for combat only at the tail end of the war, although in time to be wounded in action, my father served most of his stint during the Occupation. Lucking out, he was assigned to Supply, where he had free access to all the goodies—chocolate, coffee, toilet paper, nylon stockings, gasoline. Some of the men assigned to Supply got rich off the black market. "But," my father told me, "I was too young and too busy having fun to think of such things." There was no regret in his voice over having missed out on that particular opportunity. Instead of trading for money or gold, my father exchanged a jeep for a white horse. Other fun he had obviously included the baroness. Her inscription on the back of her photograph said something about unforgettable nights.

Before I was old enough to fully understand the fine points of reproduction, I often wished my father had married the baroness. If she had been my mother, I'd have been a junior baroness living in a castle instead of a house in the suburbs. I'd have had a glamorous life. I wanted a glamorous life. Plus, if I were a junior baroness, all the other kids would have had to curtsy at my feet. I would've liked that too.

But my father no more carried a torch for the baroness than my mother carried one for that dope-smoking, saxophone-playing boyfriend of hers. Just a few years ago, she ran into him at a hotel in Bermuda where my parents had gone for a long weekend. "I never would've recognized him," my mother told me. "He recognized me. He got fat and lost all his hair." My mother expressed gratitude that my father, although he has aged over these years—his hair's gone gray and his face lined—has held on to his good looks.

While Ruth did not succeed in breaking my parents' engagement, she did succeed in getting my mother to dislike her a lot. The dislike thrived, and eventually, having to do with a host of petty offenses, my mother came to detest the very sight of Ruth.

Six and a half years after they married, having moved from the garden apartment in Queens to a dream house in the suburbs, my parents had me. Supposedly, upon word of my birth, when the doctor said, "It's a beautiful baby girl," my father went to my mother's bedside and took her hand. "You've made me the happiest man on earth," he said. The only thing better than having my mother for his wife was to also have a replica of her in miniature for a daughter. Of course, I didn't exactly turn out that way. For one thing, I'm the spitting image of my father's sister Ruth. "But you're much prettier," my mother always adds.

I was tutored on the importance of *pretty*. In all the years I lived with my parents, I never once saw my mother in slovenly, comfortable clothes. She never donned a sweatshirt and baggy pants or a ratty old bathrobe. And each day at five-thirty, my mother went to the bathroom, where she freshened her makeup and redid her hair to look nice for my father when he got home from work. As a teenager, I berated her for this, for fussing over her looks, for pandering to the male ideal.

"I do this because *I* want to," my mother said. "*I* want to look nice for my husband."

When I was older, I came to understand again and again firsthand that passion can rapidly wane and then vanish before you know it. And I came to see the trick to my mother's fresh coat of lipstick, her dab of perfume behind her ears, was that it heightened *her* anticipation.

After having had her fill as a homemaker, my mother went back to school and became a high school English teacher. While attempting to educate young people is a noble cause, what really gave my mother a kick was to have all eyes on her, to be the center of attention. And so when it was offered to her, she bit at the opportunity to play Blanche DuBois in the school production of *A Streetcar Named Desire*. For weeks she wafted around the house drawling, "Ah always depend on the kindness of strangers." At the end of each of the four performances, my father applauded like a madman and then presented his star with a bouquet of white roses.

While my mother has acted as if the hospital bed were a prop, as if the doctors were the supporting cast, and heart surgery were the role all the great actresses dream of playing, my father sits desperate for the curtain call.

He stares at the clock, then gets up and strays from the waiting room. He is gone for maybe twenty minutes and must've been to the hospital gift shop, because he returns clutching the strings of two Mylar balloons. One reads *Get Well Soon*. The other says *I Love You*.

My father says nothing, but holds the strings as the balloons bob and duck coyly as if they were courting one another.

More than forty years married and they still hold hands when they walk, still smooch like teenagers. And I still wonder how on earth they managed to infuse ordinary lives with a grand love affair. I still wonder how it is that my father doesn't wish he'd stayed on in Europe, an expatriate riding a white horse and running around with a baroness. Why doesn't he have regrets that he came home to marry a girl from the adjacent borough, to become a good family man, a provider who went off to work each day so that they could have a house in the suburbs, two cars in the garage, and his wife could drip in gold jewelry?

And how is it that my mother, who made a spectacular Blanche DuBois, doesn't stop to mourn the life where she could have been star of stage and screen instead of wife, mother, high school English teacher?

And how is it that I, the only daughter of this union, the witness to their keen love, their wondrous love, such a love that, for them, is everything, could conclude that for me, such a love would never be enough?

T his was the question: What are we?

"We're Jewish," my mother said, "but not really." We were of Jewish descent the way some people's backgrounds were Norwegian or English. We were assimilated, unassuming. Not only didn't we observe the faith, but we'd distanced ourselves from Jewishness as if all of it—languages, culture, customs, humor—smelled of gefilte fish. No one would take us for Jews, and while we didn't deny our heritage, we didn't call attention to it either.

On a Sunday outing at the Mystic Aquarium, I saw Hasidim for the first time. Although I knew it was impolite, I could not help but stare at this family all bundled up despite the July heat. Their boy was around my age, and his sidelocks curled, sticking to his pale, pinched face. "Don't go anywhere near them," my mother admonished. "They're filthy. They don't bathe."

We celebrated Christmas, hung stockings and exchanged gifts under the tree, although we drew the line at a crèche on the lawn, and the Christmas cards my mother sent featured snowy woods. American Christmas cards that implied Jesus was someone like Johnny Appleseed.

A week before Easter, my mother bought new Easter outfits for my sister and me: puffy dresses, patent leather Mary Janes, boater hats with ribbons trailing down the back.

The following day my sister, RoseAnne, and I were left in a neighbor's care because my parents had to pay a shivah call. Daddy's great-aunt Sarah had passed away. This was how I pictured sitting shivah: grown-ups seated on blocks of ice, teeth chattering.

This neighbor took RoseAnne and me to her church for the annual Easter egg hunt. RoseAnne and I were thrilled.

Each child was given a basket lined with lime-green cellophane grass to carry the eggs we collected. At the end of an hour, whoever had the most eggs would win the giant chocolate bunny. Solid chocolate, not hollow, with a collar of lilac sugar crystals around its neck.

Ready! Set! Go! The pastor blew the whistle, and we scattered. It was as if God Himself were steering me around. Eggs, eggs everywhere. Nestled against rocks, peeking out from under foliage, revealed to me in bursts of color—blue against a tree trunk, red in the grass, yellow on asphalt. My basket overflowethed.

I'd collected the most eggs by a landslide, as the judges confirmed by counting them out. Twice. Then the judges conferred and made an announcement. While I, indeed, had the most eggs and was to be congratulated for that, I was a guest. Only a church member could get the prize. I got the same crappy handful of penny candy all the other kids got.

This was my understanding: *Guest* was a euphemism. And to be Jewish but not really meant you could partake in the Easter egg hunt, but you could not win the chocolate bunny.

the zen of driving

This is what I picture: *An expanse of highway cutting between cornfields. Kansas. The road is flat. The sky ahead is robin's-egg blue. I'm behind the wheel of a Corvette that is the same color as the sky. My Corvette is a convertible, and the interior is white. I'm coasting along at seventy, seventy-five miles per hour. I'm wearing wraparound sunglasses.*

"Give it some gas," Manny says. "Jou got to put jour foot on the gas." Manny, my driving instructor, is from the Dominican Republic. I never learned to drive before now because I'm from the Upper West Side of New York. By the time I was seven, I knew mass transit inside out. I thought the world ended at the far tip of Queens. Now, it's not that I need to drive for any particular reason, but I'm desperate to learn because I can't stop picturing it. "Gas," Manny repeats. "Jou got to go fifteen at least."

I TURN MY key in the door as if it were the ignition to a Lamborghini. *Vroom.*

"Is that you?" my husband calls out. There's no telling when Julian will, or will not, be around. He's a professor of economics and lately is home more often than not because he's taken up a hobby. Without turning to look at me, Julian asks, "How was your lesson?"

"Great," I say. "I put my foot on the gas. Manny thinks I'll be ready for the road test soon." Actually, Manny has been saying as much for quite some time, since my first lesson, which consisted of mastering the key in the ignition, mirror adjustment, buckling up my seat belt, and distinguishing the gas pedal from the brake. Manny had said, "Jou're a natural. Jou'll be taking the road test in no time."

I peek over Julian's shoulder. Set up on one of his six easels is a canvas streaked with yellow. Not one shade of yellow, but all of them: lemon yellow, cadmium yellow, yellow light, pale hue, yellow deep hue, Naples yellow, yellow ocher, raw sienna. These yellows are one in a series. Julian has done the same thing in blues: cerulean blue, cobalt blue, Prussian blue, French ultramarine. And in reds too. His next will be either greens or browns. These are not paintings. These are exercises to see the colors, to experience the sensation of tube to palette to brush to canvas. It's all quite an adventure for Julian, and he marvels at the colors as if he'd been blind since birth and now, via a miracle, is sighted.

He has been awarded a Pearl Paint Frequent Shopper Discount Card, although Julian hasn't yet painted anything other than his streaks of color. He has, however, been buying supplies to last Michelangelo two ceilings. And he's been buying books to read up on painting. Julian has books titled *Painting Trees and Flowers, Portraits in Oil, Painting Weather, Painting Landscapes, The Human Form, Painting Abstracts, The Seurat-the-Dot Method,* and *The Complete Encyclopedia of Oil Painting.* When he'd lugged that one home, I said, "Well, that's it. You won't be needing any more books on painting now." But I was wrong. I'd forgotten all about watercolors, acrylics, ink, and airbrushes.

Julian continues to play with his paints, and I go to the bedroom. Shutting the door behind me, I turn on the television but close my eyes.

This is what I picture: *The Freeway. The L.A. Freeway. On one side is the city, sprawling high-rises and shopping centers. On the other side is the ocean. The Pacific Ocean crowded with blond surfer boys wearing tropical-print trunks. I'm driving a Mustang. A '67 Mustang. Red. My fingernails are lacquered the same shade of red, and they make a jazzy contrast against the black leather steering wheel. I flick on the radio. The Beach Boys are singing, "And we'll have fun, fun, fun till your daddy takes the T-bird away."*

• • •

"DO YOU REALIZE," I say to Mark, "I've never been to a drive-in movie. Never ordered a burger and a shake from a carhop on roller skates. And I have never had sex in the backseat of a car."

"You're not missing anything." Mark glides his hand along my back. "Sex in the backseat of a car is cramped, and you bang your head on the arm rests."

We're in Mark's bed. Mark and Sally's bed to be exact, but Sally is out of town. She'll be gone for three weeks, during which I'll be in her bed four or five times more. Sally is an actress with an interpretive Shakespearean theater troupe, and often they take their show on the road. This time, they're in New Hampshire doing *Macbeth* in Kabuki makeup. The play has been edited so it's all in haiku. "That sounds positively stupid," I'd said.

The time before this one, Sally was in Maryland playing Cordelia in a rock 'n' roll version of *King Lear*. When she got back, she said to Mark, "I smell perfume on my sheets. I don't wear perfume." When he called this morning, Mark reminded me, "No perfume, remember?"

"Right," I said. No perfume, but when I got here, and we pulled at each other's clothes, a red button the size of a quarter popped off my blouse and flew under the dresser. If Sally ever sweeps back there, she'll find it.

At ten minutes to four, Mark gets out of bed and steps into his jeans. "I'll be right back," he says. "I've got to move the car." On Tuesdays and Thursdays, the car is parked in front of his building until four o'clock, when he has to move it across the street. It's a steel-blue car, a compact hatchback; not exactly a minivan, but a car that toys with the possibility of such a commitment without quite making it. It's nothing like the cars I picture. Still, I wouldn't mind driving it, but when I say to Mark, "I'll move it for you," he shakes his head. "It's Sally's car, really. Not mine."

"Yeah? So what?" It's absurd that her car should be off-limits to me, when her husband is not.

When Mark returns, I am dressed and sitting in the living room. His face registers a question, but we never talk much with our clothes on. "I have a driving lesson at five," I explain.

THIS IS WHAT I picture: *I'm driving a Jeep Cherokee along the dirt roads of Appalachia. My Jeep Cherokee moves like a tank over bumps, crags, and through the brambles.*

"Watch the curve," Manny shouts.

"What curve?" I don't see any curve.

"The curve. The curve." Manny is losing patience with me. The car rises and drops with a thump. Oh. That curve. He meant the *curb*. The sidewalk, although Manny's accent is not usually the reason for my not following him. It's that I don't listen. Like now he's telling me something about the distance between the car and the curb, but it's just static, like keeping the car in idle.

• • •

HAVING COMPLETED YELLOWS, Julian has moved on to greens. He's saving the browns for last because he read that brown is a tricky color to master. He wants to be more accomplished before he opens those tubes. "You know what I really need?" he asks, but before I can guess, he says, "A maulstick."

A maulstick is used to support and steady the artist's arm and is useful when painting intricate detail. Julian does not need a maulstick. Julian needs nothing else in the way of supplies. He has sixty-two brushes, eleven palette knives, five varieties of linseed oil. Stacks of stretched Belgium-linen canvases line our walls as if in preparation for a show, except they are blank.

While Julian examines what happens when you mix viridian green with terre verte, I open the newspaper and turn to *Automobiles for Sale*. I skim *Domestic Cars*, skip *Station Wagons and Vans* to scrutinize the *Classic Cars* column. I have every intention of buying myself a car even though Julian is dead set against it.

"Hey," I read aloud. "An Aston Martin DB4, 1960. Only seventy-two thousand dollars." I make it sound like a steal.

"The cost of the car is the least of it," Julian says. "There's insurance. A new driver pays through the nose for insurance. And upkeep. Repairs cost a small fortune. Never mind parking. You're going to have to pay plenty for a garage or kill half your day looking for a spot on the street."

I want to tell him he's wrong about that, how Mark gets

up to move Sally's car and is back before the sheets cool, but all I can say is, "It's not as difficult as you make it out to be."

"I don't understand," Julian says, "why you wouldn't simply rent a car whenever you want to go somewhere," and I snap, "For the same reason you wouldn't want to rent a maulstick." In a huff, I carry the newspaper to the bedroom, where I circle ads for cars that sound dreamy.

"TODAY," MANNY ANNOUNCES with flourish, "jou will learn the broken Ju-turn." From his jacket pocket he takes a car, a Matchbox car, and places it on the dashboard. "Ees four moves. Watch." Manny rolls the toy car forty-five degrees to the left, backs it all the way out, straightens its wheels, and off it goes. "Jou try now." Manny puts the car in my hand. It sits on my open palm, and I look at it as if it were a surprise, something like an egg. "Jou have a question?" Manny asks.

"Yeah," I say. "Is this a Corvette?"

"No. Ees a Buick."

JULIAN HAS BEGUN his first real painting of something other than streaks. The *Painting Nature* book is open to a scene of a lake, a tree in the foreground, a snowcapped mountain behind. With a charcoal stick, he copies the picture line for line. *Painting Nature*, like all the books Julian has bought, is a step-by-step guide, the adult version of the Jon Nagy Learn-to-Draw set I had as a kid: two circles connected by lines made a cylinder for the locomotive. A pair of parallel lines narrowing across the paper were tracks heading away.

"What do you think?" Julian holds the book alongside his sketch.

"They look exactly alike," I say. This delights Julian, so I don't mention that the key to painting is what you bring to it.

When I first began to picture driving, but hadn't yet realized I was the one behind the wheel, I'd said to Julian, "Let's get a car and spend the weekend coursing country roads."

"And who is going to drive this car?" Julian asked. He has a driver's license, but he hasn't driven in a dozen years. He did not agree when I suggested that once in the driver's seat, it would all come back to him.

Julian mixes cerulean blue and zinc white on his palette, aiming for the same shade as the sky in the book. "You need to add a touch of black," I tell him.

"Really? How do you know that?" Julian asks.

Before I married Julian—in fact it was the morning before our first date—I gathered up my paints, my brushes, my palette knives, my maulstick, my easel, and took all of it out to the trash barrels. I waited on the sidewalk for the garbage truck to come and collect it, to be sure these things wouldn't somehow sneak back into my apartment, into my life.

"You might want to try a dot of chrome yellow with that white," I say, offering Julian another tip, and he looks at me as if he doesn't quite trust me.

• • •

"IF YOU'RE GOING to buy a used car," Mark advises, "make sure you check for rust. And do not forget the transmission."

In that instant, I get gooey. My breath shortens, and I venture, "Say that again."

"Make sure you check for rust?" Mark is not sure what it is I want, and in practically a fit, I say, "No, no. The other thing."

"Transmission?"

"Yes, yes," I sigh. Next, I want Mark to say *carburetor*, but I'm not sure how to go about it.

WE'RE STUCK IN a traffic jam on Sixth Avenue at the corner of Thirty-third Street. My hour is nearly up, and we're boxed in.

"Stay in the right lane," Manny says, as if I could change lanes without plowing into the truck next to me. Besides, except to make a left turn, Manny has consistently forbidden me to foray into the left lane. The left lane is where you go fast, where you zip past the slowpokes, the student drivers, those who do not dare. When I picture driving, I am, always, in the left lane.

With nothing else to do while waiting for the traffic to untangle, I make eye contact with the truck driver on my left. He gives my car the once-over, as if he were checking me out and the student-driver sign on the roof of the car were the equivalent of pigtails and braces, a sign that I'm something like jailbait, trouble that's not worth it.

• history on a personal note

This is what I picture: *My DeLorean looks like the car George Jetson drove. It's black, and I'm somewhere in the Southwest tooling across the desert. My DeLorean rips through the wasteland, stirring tumbleweed, shaking needles off cacti, rattling the bleached bones on a steer. Clouds of gold dust are left in my wake.*

"Hey," the truck driver leans over and calls to me, "if you can make it out of this mess, you can drive anywhere in the world." This is like telling me to come back when I'm older, and I flash him a smile.

"On the road." Manny gets snippy. "Jou got to keep jour eyes on the road."

JULIAN CALLS TO me again. "How is it now?" He steps away from his easel and chews, in contemplation, on the end of his brush.

"Great," I say. "You're a natural."

"But what about the tree? The bark? The texture of the bark? See, there." He points to a thin, jagged line of dark brown.

"Like I could reach out and touch it," I tell him. "Now, will you leave me alone so I can get ready?"

New York State requires I take a five-hour Drivers' Ed class before I can take the road test. Not that I'm ready to take the road test, but I'm anxious to take the class because I picture the instructor to be a muscular young man, wearing tight jeans and a T-shirt, who is going to talk to me about engines. He's going to use words like *horsepower, oil changes, carburetor.*

I'm halfway out the door when Julian says, "Wait a second." He's preparing to paint leaves on his tree. He's nervous. "Suppose I mess up?"

"The beauty of oils," I tell him, "is that nothing is permanent unless you want it to be."

TWELVE STUDENT DRIVERS are crammed into a makeshift classroom in my driving school's office. I sit in the front row, notebook open, pen poised, legs crossed. My skirt rides up. I intend to excel. Seated next to me is a Puerto Rican boy, seventeen if he's a day and adorable.

Our teacher makes his way to the front of the room. He is not wearing tight jeans, but gray polyester flares hoisted closer to his armpits than to his waist. He writes his name on the blackboard: Herman Bergman. Beneath his name, he writes his credentials. Herman Bergman holds many degrees and certificates in drivers' education. "Drivers' education," he tells us, "boils down to one word. *Safety!*" Herman bangs his fist on the tabletop.

It does not appear I'm going to learn a thing about engines. I'm not going to get to hear the Puerto Rican boy say *spark plug* or *stick shift*. Herman is stuck in the safety gear, as if the only reason for driving were to get from point A to point B in one piece.

Herman relates scenarios where minor infractions of the safety code led to very bad news: a father of four who didn't buckle up on his way to work, a family who dared to go sixty on the expressway and never made it to the beach. All that remained of them was the orange plastic pail and shovel for building sand castles discovered eighteen yards away from the crunched-up station wagon. There was the teenage boy who didn't stop, a truck driver who didn't yield, and a doctor who, on his way to an emergency appendectomy, tried to beat a red light. Both doctor and patient died. Another disaster involved six nuns. The driver nun was careful, but she was not a defensive driver. The nuns ended up crippled "because she wasn't watching out for the other guy and *bam!*" Herman brings his hands climactically together, as if demonstrating a volcanic eruption.

BAM! This is what I picture: *My big, old Cadillac backfires on takeoff. My Cadillac is lemon yellow with a white vinyl roof and fins. A pair of pink, foam-rubber dice dangle from the rearview mirror. It's three, maybe four, in the morning, and I'm in the Bronx, cruising the Grand Concourse, wide, tree-lined. Streetlights arc gracefully like swans' necks, guiding me the way a lighthouse beam guides a ship. My Caddy is the only car on the road because of the hour and because that's how I picture it. The traffic lights are timed in my favor. I've got no reason to stop.*

Herman wants us to go around the room and share our driving experiences with the group. A girl with tall hair relates the escapades of her boyfriend teaching her to parallel park. I groan and roll my eyes at that cute boy next to me. This prompts him to hit Herman with a spitball.

• • •

BETWEEN KISSING MARK'S neck and his chest, I make a suggestion. "What do you say we get into that car of yours and drive off somewhere."

This is what I picture: *A parkway in New England. Vermont. It's winter. The sky is overcast, and although the road is clear, the churchyard is shrouded in virgin snow. Eighteenth-century tombstones jut out, cockeyed, like a mouthful of crooked teeth. When I was fifteen, I once kissed a boy who had teeth like that. I ran my tongue along the planes and points. I'm about to tell that to Mark, but when I look over to the passenger seat, it's vacant. I am alone, driving my Porsche, my silver Porsche, which from a distance could be mistaken for a meteor.*

"Now, now," Mark reminds me, "you know it's not my car," but the difference that makes still escapes me.

This affair with Mark was never as good as I thought it would be, never as I pictured it before it began. Sometimes it's impossible to recall exactly what I'd pictured, but I know it had to do with life-affirming sex, obsession, abandon, passion-out-of-control. Oh, we do go through the motions. We rip at each other's clothing. We pant and moan and call out when and where it's appropriate, but it boils down to this: Mark thinks foreplay is something I do to him, and I can't quite get over that he won't let me drive Sally's car.

MANNY CLUTCHES AT his heart in the aftermath of a near minor collision. "Jou got to look when jou pull out. Jou got to pay attention. Jou got to focus on what jou're doing here. Where was jour mind at?"

"Tell me the truth, Manny," I ask. "When will I be ready for the road test?"

Manny shrugs.

"LOOK. I MESSED it." Julian's having a fit like a kid who has colored beyond the line. He's holding his book out for me to see that there's no smudge on that mountain.

"I like yours better," I say. "Your smudge adds dimension, some doubt." The painting of this lake, tree, and mountain—the original—probably hangs in the lobby of a Ramada Inn.

Julian takes no heart from my observation. He wants his mountain to look exactly like the mountain in *Painting Nature,* so I show him what to do. With the tip of the palette knife, I scrape away the gray. There's not much of it. Julian paints thinly. A little turpentine lifts out any residue of the smudge. "You can paint white here now," I tell him.

Julian is blissfully happy perfecting his painting when the phone rings. I go to the kitchen to answer it.

"Can you talk?" It is Mark calling to let me know that the Kabuki *Macbeth* was such a hit, it's being held over for another week. Mark and I can romp together again sooner than we'd planned. "So," he asks, "what are you doing tomorrow?"

Tomorrow. What *am* I doing tomorrow? I pause to think about that, and this is what I picture: *I'm driving a Jaguar. Forest green. I'm coursing a mountain road. Maybe it's in the Adirondacks. Or the Alps. Or the mountain in Julian's painting. The road is narrow. On both sides, the drop is steep. On my left is* the lake. To my right is a valley strewn with cars that missed a curve. They look like litter, like soda cans tossed from speeding car windows. My Jaguar takes the turns on a wish. It's joined to the road as if making love, hugging the curves as if car and road were connected by something similar to a caress. I ease my foot down on the gas pedal and, in a flash, zoom out of sight.

Out on his sundeck, that man from next door looks up at me and waves. A real neighborly wave as if he were saying "Howdy" from across a country road. Pretending I don't see him, I turn away and tell Ross, "We have got to get window shades. Those people with the sundeck are too friendly."

Those people with the sundeck are Stacy's parents. They live in the building adjoining ours, and their deck—although a floor below—is adjacent to our kitchen and living room. It is a sundeck that could easily be mistaken for a tract house backyard. Made of redwood planks, it is cluttered with a pink plastic swing set, a rubber wading pool, a barbecue grill, an umbrella-covered patio table, a tricycle, and a miniature lawn chair, baby-bear-size. They dote on that Stacy child.

Ross goes to the window and raises a hand in greeting. "Don't encourage them," I say, but Ross only laughs as if I were being cute.

I don't know the names of Stacy's parents because Stacy refers to them only as Mama and Daddy, and that's how they refer to each other too. Stacy, however, is called by name and so often as if to reinforce it, like the child might otherwise forget what she's called. They also call her Sta-Sta and Stacy-Wacy, which makes me want to puke. Stacy is two or three or four years old. Something like that. I'm lousy at determining things about children like their ages. They're little. That's all I know.

Before Ross leaves for work, I again remind him about the shades. I've been reminding Ross about the shades since we moved in last week and saw those people out there. But, while Ross has yet to come home empty-handed, he has yet to come back with window shades either. Instead, he's been buying soft-sculpture mobiles, framed prints of Mother Goose, and a five-foot-tall stuffed monkey with glass eyes from FAO Schwarz.

I am pregnant. With child. I fell into that margin of error, those two or a half of one percent who conceive despite armored precautions, which is why we moved to this apartment. I was happy in our old apartment, the one above a transvestite bar. Ross was happy there too, until I broke the news, and just like that, our apartment wasn't fit for rats to live in. Ross nearly flew out the door in search of a place with a room for the impending baby. "And lots of sunlight," he insisted. "And near a park."

He *nearly* flew out the door to apartment hunt as opposed to *immediately* flying out only because he was too busy clapping his hands and dancing around. Ross was thrilled to the bone at the idea of a baby, and he let loose with the kind of joy that can be contagious, the sort I got swept up in because sometimes I don't think.

I pad to the kitchen. Ross's cat, Phyllis, is sitting by her bowl. Generally speaking, I object to people names for pets, dopey mutts named Ralph and black cats called Emily. Before I got knocked up, before I ever even imagined it could happen, I'd said to Ross, "What are you going to name your children then? Mittens? Fluff? Spot?" I open a can of cat food, and it reeks. My stomach heaves, but I refuse to give in to morning sickness. I turn on the radio.

When I lived in San Francisco, I had a cat. I gave Claw to the astrologer who lived down the hall because I was moving to New York. Having done Claw's chart, the astrologer determined that she and Claw were destined to be together. So it worked out neatly. Pudding was the other cat I had. Pudding went to live with a drag queen from the transvestite bar when I moved in with Ross because two cats was one cat too many. This drag queen believed she and Pudding had ruled the Nile together in a past life. "Didn't we, Pudding?" She rubbed noses with the cat. Leaving a cat with a loving home is not at all the same thing as abandoning one.

I fiddle with the radio dial for the all-news station. I listen for the weather report. For more records broken. We're having the hottest summer since 1938. Each day the mercury scurries into the nineties, and then the air just sits, moving only to come in closer. Not even the frequent thunderstorms bring reprieve, although they do break up the monotony.

The other thing I listen for is reports of mayhem. Not for wars or natural disasters, but for stories of ordinary people snapping. It's going to level off at ninety-seven, and a boy in Oklahoma went to town on his parents with a hacksaw. The neighbors are quoted as saying, "We don't understand this. He's a nice boy. A good boy. There's got to be a mistake."

I was so sure I couldn't possibly be pregnant that I missed three periods before I went to the doctor. And even then I said, "I don't understand this. There's got to be a mistake."

But there was no mistake, and I went home expecting Ross to make the right decision for me. I expected him to say, "We can't have a child. We're not ready for that. We might not ever be ready for that. We don't even like children." But because Ross didn't say anything of the kind, I also thought this might be okay after all. Then the next thing I knew, it was too late to change anything but my mind.

Stacy's father is at the patio table drinking iced tea. The newspaper is spread out before him, but he's not reading it. He's watching Stacy on the swing, beaming at her as if she were doing something of value. He's the one who stays at home minding the kid. The mother leaves for work in the morning pretty much the same time Ross does. I can't figure out if the father is on vacation or if he works at home or if he's a househusband—something I'd heard of but never quite believed was for real. Stacy finishes with the swing and gets on her tricycle. She rides in circles. On every full rotation, the wheels squeak.

Before noon, Stacy and her father go inside to escape the heat. They have air-conditioning. We do not because Ross read some harebrained magazine article about how recycled air particles are not ideal for the unborn. "But what about those of us who are already born?" I asked. "We could keel over from this heat." But all Ross said was, "You have another person to consider now."

The electric fans we do have aren't powerful enough to move the density of air. They do nothing but whir. As I can't think of anything else to do, I go back to bed and stay there, dozing on and off, until I hear Ross come in. I meet up with him in the living room and eye his shopping bags. "Shades?" I ask.

"Damn." Ross says he knew he forgot something. "And I was at the hardware store too." What Ross has bought this time is paint. Cans of water-base paint in soft pastels: pink, lavender, sky blue, pale yellow. "What color should we paint the nursery?" Ross asks, and I tell him, "I like brown."

Ross has never suggested I get the shades myself because he frets if I carry anything heavier than a glass of water. In some ways, Ross is underfoot more than Phyllis. He worries that I'll strain myself. This was also why he hounded me into quitting my job before I even began to show. I was a cocktail waitress in a blues club. In some circles, that's a glamour job. It was where Ross and I met. During the day, Ross is in market research, but at night he wanted something different.

The truth is I no longer want the window shades. Viewing Stacy from above is something I've come to do now. It's a kind of voyeurism. A sort of perversion, and while I might loathe aspects of it, I can't resist the temptation. Or maybe it's less than that, as innocent as having my own ant farm. A study with window as microscope. They—Stacy and her parents—are a constant source of irritation to me, but some irritations are irresistible, the way we scratch an itch or pick at a scab.

I DON'T KNOW whether to blame the heat or my own state of being, but my feet are so swollen I can't get shoes on at all. Not even canvas espadrilles, which means I am now barefoot and pregnant. My feet hurt too much to stand for long at the kitchen window, so I pull up a chair and sit. The cat also favors the kitchen window. Keen on direct sunlight, she curls up on the ledge to nap. I stroke her as if that's why I'm here.

Stacy's mother has been home for almost an hour when Ross comes in. Stacy's mother is not friendly the way the father is. She ignores me entirely, and I was on the verge of respecting her for that until one morning when she and Stacy bounded out onto the sundeck wearing identical outfits: denim overalls, red polo shirts, red sneakers, and blue bandannas tied at their necks. With his video camera, the father filmed them standing there, and I concluded that she must be a boob too. However, I did start paying closer attention to how they dressed as a family.

Ross finds me in the chair as if I haven't moved all day. Which maybe is the case, except now I'm smoking a cigarette. "Are you out of your mind?" Ross plucks the cigarette from my lips and drowns it under the faucet.

I continue to stare out at them, at the Stacy family. The father is at the grill tending to steaks. The mother sets the table while Stacy buzzes around each parent like a yellow jacket at a picnic. "Look," I say to Ross. "Look at her. They've got her in a sailor costume. With a sailor cap. She looks like an idiot."

Ross bends at the waist to look out the window. "Oh, how adorable. And how perfect. Wait here. I've got something for you."

Ross returns from the living room with a gift-wrapped box. "Open it," he instructs. "Go on."

Ross has bought me a tiny pair of blue jeans and scaled-to-egg-size basketball high-tops. Like something from a circus sideshow, these clothes are too small to be anything but disturbing. They're queer and warped, and Ross asks, "Aren't you going to have fun dressing the baby?"

I once saw a lady on *A Current Affair* who dressed birds in period costumes: parrots in pirate outfits, a cockatoo in a Gay Nineties gown and plumed hat, a pigeon wearing a constable's uniform. It was all horrible. I stand up, and the little freak outfit falls from my lap to the floor. It gets stepped on as I brush past Ross and again as Phyllis tramples over it on her way to the litter box.

Ross follows me to the couch and incorrectly decides that this is a good time to lecture me about the hazards of smoking. "Smoking can cause birth defects," he quotes the surgeon general.

"That's it," I say. "Birth defects. My lungs can turn to tar and ash for all you care."

"Now you know that's not true. I care."

"You care only about the damn baby." I start to cry. "Baby this and baby that." This isn't the sort of crying that'll bring me relief when it's done. It's a feeble demonstration of how I feel, is all. What I really want to be doing is tearing things apart, wrecking it all, bringing down the walls to this apartment and to my life so that I can start over. I sit and snivel and could use a tissue. Ross makes a move to hug me, and in a fresh rush of anger, I fling myself to the floor. I beat at the parquet with my fists. The cat, like in a cartoon, pricks up her ears and makes a mad scramble for cover. I kick and weep and scream at Ross. Unable to articulate just how hot and sore and miserable I am, I howl like an animal.

"Shhh," Ross says. "The windows are open. They can hear you."

This is, most likely, the reason Stacy's mother ignores me. I throw these fits kind of regularly, and sometimes when I do, she hustles Stacy inside even if they're in the middle of dinner.

I scream louder and shriek a few obscenities to boot. Ross coos, "There, there. Don't cry," but it's only from exhaustion that I stop. It's too damn hot to carry on. I lie still on the floor until the aroma from their barbecued steaks snakes through our window, and Ross teases me, "They were going to invite us to dinner, but now they won't because they think you're insane."

Stacy's parents are closer in age to Ross than to me, and despite his teasing, Ross had entertained ideas about being friends with them. Get invited to their barbecues, get tips on Pampers and pureed peas, discuss toilet training. Ross and I don't have any friends. Not anymore. When I'd introduced him to my favorite friend, Lily had said, "Gee, if I'd known, I'd have fixed you up with my father." Ross's chums elbowed him in the ribs about me and made comments as if I were a dish of after-dinner mints that Ross should pass around. And so Ross and I found ourselves alone. With his cat. We're as self-contained as a one-act play.

I never wanted to make friends with Stacy's parents, and by the Fourth of July, even Ross had to admit they couldn't be anything more to us than a curiosity. Their sundeck was done up with red, white, and blue streamers. Stacy clutched a dime-store flag. Ross sat at the kitchen table while, from the window, I watched the Fuji blimp float overhead.

"Look, Sta-Sta," Stacy's father broke the calm. "A dirigible. Can you say *dirigible*?"

"Why does the kid have to say dirigible?" I asked Ross. "Why can't the kid say *blimp*?"

Ross had no idea why the kid had to say *dirigible,* and he looked so sad about it that I went to him and put my hand on his. "They're not for us," I said. "They'd make us sick."

MY BELLY GROWS the way a zucchini does. Overnight, and I can't get into any of my clothes. I'm frantically pulling things from the closet when Ross goes and gets me a pair of his chinos and one of his T-shirts. "I'll take the morning off," he tells me. "And we'll get you some maternity things, okay?"

The store is air-conditioned, and I can't help but ask Ross if he'd like me to hold my breath for the baby's sake. He gives me a look, and we sit on chairs that seem too dainty to support me. The saleswoman brings dresses over for my inspection. Ridiculous dresses. One perky getup after the next, each featuring puffed sleeves or bows or oversize buttons, as if pregnant women are themselves giant, bloated babies. I wave each dress away, and I start to cry and I continue to cry until she brings me a sailor outfit. It's the same sailor outfit the Stacy child has. Minus the cap. And, of course, bigger. This makes me laugh, and my laughter pleases Ross and the saleswoman until they realize I can't stop. I'm hysterical. Ross pats me and apologizes to the saleswoman all at once.

In the taxi, I quiet down and tell Ross we should forget about maternity clothes. "It's not like I go anywhere," I say. "I can wear your old things around the house."

The cab drops me off and heads east to take Ross to work. By the time I get inside, perspiration is dripping down my back. I try to remember the cool of the maternity shop, but I can't. I think that this weather has got to break. It's got to break or I will.

As if I'd been heard, the sky blackens. Thunder rumbles. I go around the apartment shutting windows, and just in time. The first bolt of lightning is a doozy. It breaks apart the sky and wakes the cat, who slinks off under the bed. The drops of rain are large, and they splat against the window, and then the rain comes like a pipe bursting. Fast and furious. But it's the gusts of wind that are most impressive. Gusts I imagine I can see, as if they gather volume in their strength. Unmanned, Stacy's tricycle races across the deck and dashes against a guardrail before flipping on its side. Her wading pool picks up a surf, but it's the crash of the swing set that brings Stacy's father out into the storm. He's got the idea of setting the swings upright, but that could be a task for Sisyphus. Each time he gets the swing set up, the winds knock it to the ground.

Even with my windows shut, I can hear the next gust of wind coming. This one picks up the umbrella-covered patio table. Stacy's father chases after it, diving to grab it by one leg just before it would've gone over the edge and crash-landed on the street.

He's drowning out there. Rushing to and fro and around in circles, dodging lightning bolts, trying to pin things down, hold them back as if they were time. I half hope for him to be picked up and carried away like Dorothy in *The Wizard of Oz*. But the storm doesn't last long enough for that. The wind dies to a standstill. The last few drops of rain melt away, then the clouds disperse. Within moments, it heats up again, only now it's worse because of the humidity.

Later, when I return to the window, all is right with the sundeck. Over dinner I tell Ross about the mess that was out there. I describe how Stacy's father raced around like a wet and headless chicken trying to keep their things from being carted off by the wind, but all Ross says is "Oh, right. We did get a storm. I was so busy, I forgot about it. You did remember to shut the windows in the nursery, didn't you?" Ross has painted the nursery pale yellow. He plans to paint bunnies on one wall and a garden on another.

· · ·

IT'S SORT OF interesting how I can spend my days doing absolutely nothing. I gurgle in the sun. I get cooed at by Ross. All unhappiness is expressed with a wail and some tears. And in the afternoons, I nap. It's some kind of dirty trick nature plays, reducing me to infantile ways so when the baby comes, we'll be synchronized like clocks.

I go to get a glass of juice, and the late-afternoon sun reflecting off the white kitchen walls is blinding. That kind of sunlight gives me a headache, and I would've gone directly back to the bedroom had I not heard Stacy whine magnificently, "Dad-deee, I want to take off my bathing suit." I stop dead in my tracks.

Stacy's father looks up at me. I suppose I shouldn't be so obvious. I should at least sidestep and peer out the window the way old women do from behind lace curtains. But I don't.

Turning back to his child before she does something rash, Stacy's father says, "No, Stacy-Wacy." His singsong voice is meant to convey the following: There's nothing at all wrong with Stacy-Wacy's desire to peel off her bathing suit and rub her naked little self all over Daddy's legs. Stacy's not to think there's anything dirty about wanting to seduce Daddy. But, at the same time, she must not do it because it's filthy and could mess the kid up plenty.

This dicey moment in Stacy's development promises to be a good show, so I pull up my chair. It's got to be difficult for him, this balancing act, walking the tightrope to a healthy sexuality for his daughter's future, especially while being spied on by his neighbor whom he suspects of being unhinged.

"I have an idea." He's all bright-eyed with phony enthusiasm. "Let's go on the swing. Daddy will push you. Whee!"

"No." Stacy's got another sort of Whee! on her mind. "I want to take it off." Stacy jiggles and snorts with desire as she tugs at her bathing suit straps.

Stacy's not the only one of us who has toyed with the idea of seducing her father.

She refuses the stuffed toy he offers her. It is as foolish an attempt at diversion as is trying to work up excitement for her tricycle. That it's too chilly out to take off her bathing suit is such a stupid lie that even Stacy gives it no credence.

Her father is kind of cute. In a harmless sort of way.

If things had been different, I might've whistled out the window for him, and we could've humped away these hot summer mornings. But now, seduction is out of the question. Not only do I look grotesque, but men are soft with admiration. Men seem to think that all pregnant women are involved in something sacred, holy. Take Ross—he used to be a very hot guy, but now his kisses are chaste little nothings and rough stuff's out of the question.

Such a persistent child, Stacy manages to undo the knot in the back of her suit. Slowly, as if she instinctively knows that stripping is an art form not to be hurried, the Stacy child rolls down the top of her bathing suit. In spite of, or because of, her father's pleas to stop, she giggles and thrusts out her bare chest. Stacy's father loses his cool. He shouts, "Stop that!" and raises one hand to swat Stacy-Wacy's bottom, when a furtive glance up at me in the window spares Stacy from the future association of spanking with arousal. Utterly frustrated, Stacy's father drags his daughter inside and slams the door.

R O S S   A N D   I are in bed watching the educational channel. I feel the baby kick but keep quiet about it. I pay close attention to the documentary instead. It's on the lions of the Serengeti. The stark landscape is dotted with acacia trees, and I watch how the breeze rustles across the plain the way a wildfire would. I try not to watch the lions, but Ross keeps pestering me to comment on the lioness licking her cub clean. "Isn't it wonderful?" Ross is all worked up over the maternal instinct of lions.

"Some animals," I tell him, "devour their young. Fish do it constantly. Poop out a load of little fish, turn right around, gobble up every last one, and then face front again as if nothing had happened. Nothing at all."

"You'll see," Ross says. "You're going to be a fantastic mother." But he sounds as if he were trying to convince himself of this as much as me. He's not confident.

Too uncomfortable to properly sleep, I drift in and out of consciousness. The cat is sitting sphinxlike on my chest as if she were an oracle with a message for me. I wait for it, but Phyllis doesn't so much as blink. I push her off me and go to the living room.

In the halo of moonlight, I make out a silhouette on the sundeck below. It's Stacy's parents. Locked in an embrace.

He's holding her from behind, her head nestled on his shoulder; they're looking up at the night sky. She turns, and they kiss, and this small kiss, as light but as significant as a butterfly, makes me ache.

"There you are." Ross has gotten up from bed and is almost at my side. "Are you okay? You're not sick or anything?"

"I'm fine." I tell him to go back to bed. I don't want Ross to see Stacy's parents like this. It's my secret.

THEY'RE GOING AWAY. I watch them load up the car with suitcases, tennis rackets, a Styrofoam cooler, and toys. Stacy carries her own suitcase. It has Donald Duck's face on it.

Although no one is there, I find myself looking out at the sundeck anyway. I knew about the fish eating their babies because I once kept guppies. When they all died, it took me weeks to dispose of the fish tank. I watched it empty save for the tiny plastic scuba diver blowing bubbles from the pump.

I find myself wondering where the Stacy family has gone, and I think about how funny it would be if I were to show up there. If I could rent a room a floor above theirs, and from my balcony overlooking the ocean, I could watch them frolic on the beach.

On day three of their disappearance, I start to wonder if they're gone for good. That they did not go on vacation, but rather moved away, leaving the swings, the wading pool, the umbrella-covered patio table, for the next family to move right in, the way a lost soul will inhabit a sleeping body. I discover that I am upset. I don't want another family. I want the Stacy family.

Another day passes, and I've nearly given up hope of ever seeing them again when their car pulls up in front of their building. I rush as best as I can, which, at this point, is no more than a hurried waddle, to Ross and I give him the news. "They're back."

"Who's back?"

"The Stacy family. They've come back."

Ross looks at me funny and asks, "Why do you care?" and I deny that I do.

THE CAT EDGES around me for a spot on the windowsill. Stacy's father is hosting a hen party for some other househusbands and their children. As if I were hallucinating, I so crisply picture these men wearing aprons and women's shoes. They're drinking iced tea with mint sprigs and eating brioches, which Stacy's father must've picked up at the corner bakery, although I prefer to think that he baked them himself. While they chat, the fathers keep a collective eye on the wading pool, where the children plop and splash.

Above the din I hear a piercing screech. "Miiiine!" Stacy snatches a rubber boat from a round-headed boy. Clutching the boat, she scoops up all the floating toys, hoarding them, selfish little beast that she is. Her father excuses himself from the table and goes poolside, where he gives Stacy a lecture on sharing.

My phone rings, and I answer it without turning from the window. It's Ross telling me he has to work late. "I'm sorry," he says. "Why don't you call someone, a friend, and go out to dinner tonight?"

The fathers are packing up their belongings. I hang up the phone without responding to Ross's suggestion. Bottles, diapers, rattles, get loaded into Danish bookbags. Stacy won't have to share her toys, after all. The other children are going home maybe because it's nap time, or maybe because the fathers want to get back for their favorite soap operas. Or maybe because they want to get their kids away from Stacy.

When they've gone, when Stacy has no one to pester, she seems disoriented. She spins around as if blindfolded for a game of pin the tail on the donkey. She goes in circles, then comes to a halt looking up at my window. "Kitty!" she squeals.

For the first time ever, Stacy has noticed the cat, much the same way the cat will suddenly spot a smudge on the wall—one that's always been there but, for whatever reason, escaped her attention—and mistake it for a fly. "Kitty!" Stacy's got a pudgy index finger aimed at Phyllis.

Stacy's father kneels next to her so that they are close in height. "Yes," he says. "Kitty. Pretty kitty."

"Kitty cat." Stacy claps and bounces like she's got to go to the bathroom. Her delight over Phyllis is by no means mutual. The cat yawns and looks past the child and her father. "I want kitty cat," Stacy demands. "Give me kitty."

Her father does say no, but so softly, so apologetically, it is a no without meaning. Stacy repeats, "Give me kitty."

"But that's her kitty." Stacy's father is referring to me. He could not really think that his child would care that the cat is mine. Not this child. "I want kitty cat." Stacy gears up for a tantrum.

I could give the cat to her. I could call down to her father and say, "I'm going to be moving, and I can't take the cat with me. If you promise to give Phyllis a loving home, Stacy can have her." But this time, I'm not going to do that. I place my hand on the cat's head, not to pat her, but possessively. Stacy, ignoring her father's gentle reasoning, cries out, "Give me kitty!"

I scoop the cat up in my arms, and together we leave my place at the window.

exclusive pleasures

Try this as an experiment: Invite my mother to lunch. On exquisite bone-china plates, serve Kibbles 'n Bits. Garnish with a sprig of fresh parsley. Watch my mother smile politely, if not painfully, as she eats. Listen to her say, "Hmmmm, delicious." She will also say, "You must give me the recipe." My mother will eat all the dog food on her plate save for one bite. The remaining forkful is left to let the hostess know that the meal was both yummy and sufficient.

This experiment can be replicated with my sister, the statistical variation being that RoseAnne won't eat more than one bite of Kibbles. RoseAnne never eats more than one bite of anything. She considers eating to be vulgar. RoseAnne believes it is elegant to suppress all appetites.

My sister is emaciated, concave in the belly and chest. She hasn't any hips either. Her legs are like broomsticks. She eats enough to stay alive but not enough to live.

Our mother is plucky with pride over how RoseAnne turned out to be so delicate. Such fine manners. Such self-control, she doesn't even menstruate.

Rather than being unnerved by the fact that, at age twenty-seven, she no longer gets her period, my sister is smug that her body has the decency to refrain from something icky. Instead of buying tampons, once a month RoseAnne goes to a salon to get her body waxed. Other than what's on her head, she's as hairless as a cue ball.

Of RoseAnne, it has never been said that she is too smart for her own good. My sister graduated, barely, from a junior college which is another name for a finishing school. I believe she majored in Calligraphy and Flower Arrangements.

When we were young, staying up past our bedtime to watch the late movie, I dreamed of being Liz Taylor or Sophia Loren, of wearing a tattered slip and having a heaving bosom with cleavage to hell and back. RoseAnne wanted to be Audrey Hepburn.

Although I can picture RoseAnne having sex, what I can't picture is RoseAnne having fun having sex. RoseAnne is headache prone, and when, some ten years back, she told me that she'd given up her virginity, she phrased it like this: *Last night, I was deflowered.*

Deflowered—plucked, and then you die from anguish. A year later, when it was my turn to get laid, I'd said, "Hey,

RoseAnne. I lost my cherry." And my sister said, "It's disgusting the way you always talk about food."

Now that I think of it, you never saw Audrey Hepburn sit down to a good meal. On the other hand, Liz Taylor could devour a turkey leg like she was Henry VIII.

I look at my sister, her face sinking into itself—which my mother sees as RoseAnne's gorgeous cheekbones—and I call to her across the table, "Hey, Rosie."

RoseAnne looks up from her dinner—two slices of cucumber on a bed of watercress. To be called Rosie sets her teeth on edge.

"You know, Rosie," I say, "I think you're putting on some weight. You're looking a little *zoftig* there." I cup my hands in front of my breasts. Then, I sit back and watch my sister panic, groping at her body, feeling for flesh, for Jew meat you can't starve off no matter that you never eat more than one bite.

Jerking off is not onomatopoeic for women the way it is for
men. Men get all sorts of clever and amusing names for it.
Names that sound like fun. Men get to beat the meat, flog the
dong, stroke the jones, blast the shaft, spank the monkey,
climb the flagpole, hob the knob, and date Rosy Palm.

"True," I tell Irving, "there are limitations to the vocabu-
lary, but I've got more options in the act. Where it counts."

Irving calls my options "multitudes in the valley of decision." Irving thinks he's a card.

It's not that I don't like having sex with men, because I do.
Sex with men can be very nice, but when I have sex with
myself, I *never* miss. Masters and Johnson, people who knew,
said that, for women, not only is the self-induced orgasm

more intense, but masturbating women enjoy many sequential orgasms and that usually physical exhaustion alone terminates an active masturbatory session. In other words, to have sex with myself is to hit the jackpot.

"So why bother with men at all?" Irving asks, and I say, "Because I can't go down on myself, that's why."

Still, this business of flying solo is a mixed bag, and I'm unable to reduce it to the essentials. Oh, to be a pond snail, hermaphroditic and choiceless. However, I don't dare let Irving in on any ambivalence. For Irving, I am cavalier without conflict, a bawdy libertine.

I can't tell if Irving buys my bravado or not. His face is impassive. Enigmatic. A Jewish sphinx. "Such a *yentzer* in the head I never met in my life," Irving says. "*Farschtejst yentzer?*" He translates, "A sexual athlete. A Mickey Mantle of the genitals."

Irving was my husband's suggestion.

Eugene had said, "Maybe you ought to see somebody."

AT A CROWDED party in a house in Bedford, I found my husband Eugene in a far corner of the kitchen necking with a blonde. His eyes were shut. I watched him fumble with her breasts before I went and locked myself in the bathroom. Perched on the edge of the tub, I imagined myself sitting in a tufted chair, smoking cigarettes and watching Eugene and the blond babe go at it. When that picture got dull, I switched channels as if I were watching television.

After adjusting my panties, I washed my hands. For form,

in case someone was out there waiting, I flushed the toilet. Then, I went and got Eugene. I took him by the elbow and said, "Let's go home, Eugene. You're drunk. You don't know what you're doing."

Eugene dozed while I drove back to the city.

The next morning I woke to an apologetic Eugene between my legs. I lifted my head and looked down at him, as if to check on who was there. Then, my head rested back on my pillow, and the nicer this all felt, the less I connected it with Eugene. In my mind, whoever it was resembled Mr. Clean of liquid-detergent fame. The bald guy with the Incredible Hulk muscles who wears a white T-shirt and a gold earring. Only my Mr. Clean neither smiled nor winked, but I did give him an eyepatch.

"AN EYEPATCH?" IRVING finds this detail to be significant. He coaxes me into remembering that when I was five or six, I got aroused by Captain Hook from *Peter Pan*. Around that same time, I got a blue plastic record player along with a collection of LPs for young listeners, one of which was sea chanteys. What fortune! In my bedroom, I took off my clothes and danced naked to "Blow the Man Down." I gyrated and shimmied, shaking my six-year-old booty for the pirates as they drank rum and sang, "Come all ye young fellows who follow the sea."

• • •

I CANNOT GET Eugene back into focus. Each time we have sex, I imagine him to be someone or something else. I've had Eugene as my grade-school principal, Eugene as Chinese emperor from the Tang dynasty, Eugene as physician, Eugene as seven bikers. And still, even with all that, sex with Eugene leaves me hanging. Wanting. For satisfaction, I have sex with myself. There is no sign of Eugene then either. Not so much as a cameo appearance, and I'm doing myself a lot. It has become a hobby. What I do in my spare time.

Masturbation is supposed to be a poor substitute. Something teenage boys and nuns do. Filler. In lieu of a steady bang. Those of us getting regular pooch are not supposed to be fishing around in our own pants, are we?

It occurs to me that I married a sexual lemon.

It also occurs to me that I'm a pervert.

"IT'S ALMOST AS if men are foreplay," I tell Irving. "Do you think maybe I'm a pervert?" I say *pervert* like it's a really cool thing to be.

"Nah," Irving says. "A little *meshuga* maybe. But not a pervert."

IT IS MY job to make dinner because I get home from work an hour before Eugene does. Although I really don't see what that has to do with it. I go in an hour earlier, and he doesn't make breakfast. But, here I am, making the salad for dinner, and I get a cucumber from the refrigerator. A sizable cucumber, and it brings James to mind. The first time I saw James's cock, I drew in a deep breath. I understood phallic worship. I wanted to genuflect in its presence. But I never gave it the kind of stature James gives it.

James thinks that big cock of his is the be-all and the end-all, which is one of the ways he reveals that he's a chuckle-head. It is an impressive cock, but regardless, sex with James must be choreographed. As if getting him from the Lower East Side to the Lincoln Tunnel, I direct, "More. There. No, here. To the left. Lower. Harder. Deeper." But the very miserable part is that no sooner do I say, "Yes. Yes, that's it," does James let go. Then he asks, "Was it good for you too?"

This cucumber has it over on James, and it isn't going to slip in on its own. Even with James the first few times, we needed lubricant. We used suntan oil. I hoist myself up on the butcher-block counter and reach for the tub of garlic butter.

Voilà! and after all that, the cucumber goes in the garbage disposal and Eugene comes home from work. Sniffing around the kitchen, he asks, "Did you make garlic bread?"

Over dinner, I ask Eugene to pass the salt. I ask if his steak is well done enough. Then I ask, "Was there ever a time in your life when you jerked off a lot?"

"You bet." Eugene warms with the memory. "When I was a kid. Fourteen. Fifteen. I spent days at a clip pulling my pud raw over *Playboy* centerfolds, *National Geographic*, the Sears catalog. Bras and girdles, you know. Eventually all the pages would get stuck together. Why do you ask?"

"No reason," I say. "Just curious. What about girls? Do you think girls masturbate much?"

"For Christ's sake," Eugene says. "We're eating."

MY ADVENTURE WITH the cucumber transforms the Korean vegetable market on my block into an erotic boutique. Like Pavlov's dog, I can't pass by without getting wet. The vegetable bin in my refrigerator has become a pleasure dome, bountiful with zucchini, cucumbers, corn on the cob, and an occasional freak potato. Vegetables stay hard for days. A zucchini never asks for a back rub. A carrot couldn't care less if I smoke when we're done.

"BUT THE BEST part," I tell Irving, "is that no vegetable asks if it was good for me too."

"You're *shtupping* vegetables? Why not a vibrator? What gives with the vegetables?" Irving asks. He does, however, concede to me the corn on the cob, nubby kerneled and mythologically substantive.

"Vegetables," I tell Irving, "are not stand-ins. But a battery-operated penis is. Plastic." I scrunch my nose.

"You'll pardon me"—Irving's voice is as dry as sand—"I didn't know it made a difference what you stick up yourself had to be of natural fibers."

What I don't tell Irving is that you can't put a battery-operated vibrator down the garbage disposal. If I couldn't grind up the evidence, I'd be faced with it.

SHORTLY AFTER I found Eugene necking with the blonde at the party in Bedford, I read to him from a *Dear Abby* column. Eugene was watching television when I said, "Listen to this. This woman writes that during sex with her husband, she has lesbian fantasies. She's concerned. She's signed the letter *Am I Queer?* Dear Abby advises her to go with it. Fantasy is perfectly natural. What do you think Dear Abby fantasizes about?"

And Eugene said, "I think you ought to see someone."

I thought he meant "see someone" as in "see someone else, have an affair." I was already seeing someone—James—but then Eugene clarified, "Someone you can talk to."

FOR MY WEEKLY sessions with Irving, I doll up. As if to bring pizzazz to his daily chore of hearing out reams of petty human miseries. Against the couch of field-mouse brown, I look as out of place here as an anachronism.

Irving has white hair in need of a trim, and the chair he sits in is one of those Scandinavian jobs that I associate with people who wear socks with sandals. Often, Irving speaks to me in Yiddish, which I don't much understand, but I'm convinced the words are trinkets and baubles spoken to delight me. On a glass coffee table, next to a box of Kleenex, is a bowl of fruit. Always. Today there are two tangerines, some pears, and a banana.

I MEET VIOLET for lunch. We work for different companies but we're both in the vicinity of Rockefeller Center. Violet and I claim to keep no secrets from each other, but we do. For instance, Violet knows about James but not about the majesty of his cock. I did tell her that I found Eugene necking with a blonde at a party, to which she said, "What the hell were you doing in Bedford?" I did not tell her the other part, how this prompted a visit to the bathroom to pleasure myself. All I said was, "Someone from Eugene's office had a birthday party." I also said, "He should've had the decency to do it behind my back."

When we were in college together, Violet talked me into peeing against a tree. With her. The two of us peeing against a tree. She said it was that which made boys such good friends. How boys achieve a camaraderie rare in women. "Men claim it's the army or the locker room," Violet said. "But that's not it. They bond by peeing together on trees."

Over lunch I ask Violet to pass the salt. I ask her how is that chicken salad, and then I ask her, "Do you masturbate much?"

Violet turns crimson. "What kind of question is that?"

"I thought we had no secrets." Then I shake my head as if to say, *It figures*. "Boys talk about jerking off constantly. They even do it in front of each other. No wonder men have achieved a camaraderie rare in women. Look how prissy we get over the subject."

I am as successful in my manipulation of Violet as I am in the other kind, and she tells me about her weekend in Vermont with someone called Walter. "His underwear had holes in it," Violet says. "And it wasn't entirely clean either, if you get my drift. And if that weren't wretched enough, we watched John Wayne movies on television. There's a connection there," Violet tells me. "Anyway, I just couldn't get past the underwear. During the drive home, I was tired and I wanted to nap so I climbed into the backseat of the car, and I did it. You know, what you asked about. It. Right there in the backseat of Walter's Volvo while he was driving along I-95. When I came, I cried."

"You cried?" I ask. "Why?"

"I don't know. I guess the whole weekend was a disappointment. So what about you?" Violet returns the serve. "Do you do it much?"

"No," I say. "Never."

There's a practical joke I've heard tell of where a group of boys propose to the new kid on the block that they engage in a circle jerk. So they all sit in a circle, lights out. Once in the dark the boys do no more than unzip their flies and make the appropriate noises. Only the new kid really goes for it, and when he shoots his load, he finds himself in the spotlight, spent pud in his hand, jizz on the floor, and the other boys laughing all over themselves. I treat Violet to lunch because I feel like a bit of a heel, as if I've played a practical joke on her.

•   •   •

"DO YOU LIKE John Wayne?" I ask Irving.

"Who?" Irving says. "Who's John Wayne? Oh, you mean the cowboy? Nah. Such *chozzerai*."

I tell Irving about Violet, about how after she masturbated, she cried, and he asks me, "Do you ever cry after?"

"No," I say. "Never."

It is true. I don't shed tears, but there are moments of melancholy, weighted with grief. Postcoital *tristesse* without the coital, and then the desire to weep fades the way a dream does.

Irving makes a note on his pad like he's Saint Peter at the gate or Santa checking his list. Then Irving asks if I am familiar with the story of Lilith. "Lilith was the first woman," he tells me. "Before Eve. She was also made from clay. Just like Adam. Therefore when Adam requested that Lilith lie on the ground so he could mount her, she very nicely told Adam he could get down on the dirt himself, thank you very much. Not that Lilith wasn't interested in fooling around," Irving footnotes. "She just didn't go in for the missionary position. Well, Adam, who we know wasn't always the brightest bulb, insisted and still Lilith refused. After a little while of this back-and-forth, Lilith grew furious. She uttered some magic words which lifted her into the air, and off she went, leaving Adam without a girlfriend. So God stepped in, and He dispatched some angels to find Lilith and bring her back to Adam." Irving stops and folds his hands as if that were the end of the story.

"Well?" I want to know. "Did the angels find her?"

"Oh, yes. They found her by the Red Sea where she was cavorting with demons and devils."

I make mention that the Red Sea sounds as if it were the precedent for Club Med, and Irving says, "Exactly. And Lilith knew as much too. She asked the angels how, after all this, could they possibly expect her to return to Adam and live like a housewife. It's not possible. And that's when God made Eve."

"But what happened to Lilith?" I ask.

"It's not important," Irving says. "Let it suffice to say that Lilith had a full life of a different nature."

JAMES IS A musician and a waiter, which was how I met him less than a year into my marriage. He had asked me, "Do you want dressing on the side?" and I said, "Yes."

James does not take seriously my request that he play with his saxophone in a way that he has never done before. "Yeah, I'll fuck you with my horn, baby." He waves his cock around as if that were the instrument of my choice.

"HE'S A BIT of a *putz*, the boyfriend?" Irving refers to James as "the boyfriend," which sounds silly to me, and *lover* is a word that gives me the creeps, which is something Irving finds curious. He wonders if it's the very intimacy of the word that disturbs me, and I say, "Could be." Regardless, it doesn't adequately describe James. For James, I use the word *paramour. Paramour* I like. Love on the side. Come to think of it,

Eugene is also love on the side. Only I am the main event, and I tell Irving, "I've quit having fantasies."

"Impossible," Irving says. "You shut your eyes. You must be thinking of something."

"But I'm not shutting my eyes. I'm keeping them open to watch myself in the mirror. My flesh. My breasts. My thighs. My fingers. My toenails painted red like rosebuds."

"Ah," Irving says. "Your eyes shall be opened and ye shall be as gods."

"Yes. That's it exactly. I'm the star in my own blue movie."

IN HIS BED, while he eats chocolate ice cream from the container, I tell James that I want to give him a demonstration, like I am a vacuum cleaner salesman.

"Why in the world would I want to watch you get yourself off?" James's lower lip is rimmed with chocolate. "That's dykey."

NOW EUGENE WANTS me to quit seeing Irving. He complains that it is too much of an expense, a waste of good money.

I call Eugene a *shnorrer*, which might or might not be the right word for him, but no matter because he doesn't know Yiddish at all.

"That's another thing," he says. "You're drifting away from me. It's like sometimes you're not there."

"I know exactly what you mean," I tell him. "Sometimes it's like you're not there either."

" I N A W A Y ," I tell Irving, "I feel sorry for James. He has no idea what's been lost. If he had watched me, we would've found faith. The sort of faith that comes from having witnessed a miracle."

"And which miracle did you have in mind?" Irving asks. "The burning bush but the bush is not consumed?"

I laugh. "That's a good one, Irving."

"How nice for you that you're enjoying yourself. But tell me, what are you going to do now?"

"I don't know. Maybe have another affair. Try my luck elsewhere."

Irving tells me that King Solomon had seven hundred wives and three hundred concubines, but it's unclear what Irving is driving at. I wait for a hint, but he's not giving one. I'd never want to get into a poker game with Irving.

"So," I venture, "are you saying that salvation is in numbers?"

"No. I'm telling you that his wives turned away his heart."

"Yeah? So? Big deal. He still had the harem."

"Big deal? Do you have any nerve endings, any soft spots, other than those of the erogenous zones?" I have never seen Irving angry before. He does not shout or bang his fist. "Big deal?" His is the even-toned, ominous fury of the Jewish God; the sort of anger that lets you think you're in deep trouble.

"What are you going to do?" I ask. "Cast me out?"

"Too easy." Irving dismisses banishment as not sufficient. "You're going to get down to *geshefte*," and I'm wondering if that means down on my knees when Irving says in English, "Business. Quit the jerking off here."

"Quit? What do you mean quit?"

"Here in my office where you masturbate without your hands, where you fabricate sin, where you brag. That jerking off." Irving leans forward out of his Scandinavian chair, and sweetly now, as if he's concerned that something will break apart, he says, "I don't buy the bravado."

I feel as if Irving has invaded something private. I feel as if I am exposed, and I want to cover up but I don't know which body parts are involved. Instead, I reach into the fruit bowl and chose a plum. I hold it in my hand, not sure what to do next, until Irving tells me, "Go ahead. Eat, darling. Eat."

the cape man

He wore a black cape, and the palms of his hands were painted silver. Some reports said his face was painted silver too. At night—the Cape Man came out only after dark—he crept around in our backyards and up to our windows, pressing his silver hands against the glass.

Everyone knew someone who'd seen the Cape Man, although no one had seen him themselves. But he was there. Out there. And he had to be up to something dreadful, otherwise why would he cloak himself in a black cape in summer and go slinking around people's yards at night, peering into windows?

During the day, like a bat, the Cape Man slept in the

Aqueduct. Three blocks from my house, the Aqueduct was a dirt road leading to the water tower. On both sides were trees, vines, brambles, and raspberry bushes. Black-eyed Susans grew wild, and there was a stream where you could sometimes find salamanders. Mr. Cypik, who lived on the next block from us, committed suicide by hanging himself from the water tower. In the morning, on the way to work, to school, to shopping, everybody saw him up there swinging from a rope. They shielded the sun from their eyes and squinted up at him, but it took a while before anyone realized it was Mr. Cypik. They thought he was just some old rags that probably Artie Junot tossed up there. Artie Junot was a troublemaker, and suicide wasn't something our neighbors did, although one winter Mrs. Osborne ran out of her house and down the street naked, pulling clumps of hair from her head.

The police came to my house to talk to my parents about the Cape Man. They were, they said, checking into the situation. Every year my parents bought tickets to the Policemen's Ball, but they never went to it. I began to doubt there even was a Policemen's Ball and suspected it was like when Kevin Robison collected money in a can for Catholic orphans but used the orphans' money to buy a comic book that showed Popeye and Olive Oyl having sex. He bought the comic book from Artie Junot. Artie Junot had a stack of those comics. Some were of Betty Boop. The police told my parents that, to the best of their knowledge, there was no Cape Man, but they would continue their investigation of the alleged sightings.

Elizabeth Langly saw the Cape Man, but I didn't know

whether to believe her because she was deformed and told a lot of lies. Mrs. Langly tried to buy friends for her daughter. Sometimes I played with Elizabeth to get toys and candy.

When Skipper, Barbie's kid sister, hit the stores, I got one. I would've thought Pammy Barnett would get one too because Skipper didn't have breasts. That's why Pammy couldn't have Barbie. Her mother said Barbie gave kids ideas. All of Pammy's dolls were the kind for display only, porcelain babies dressed in ornate velvet-and-lace outfits that were glued on. They were pretty to look at, but you couldn't play with them.

My parents didn't believe in the Cape Man, but we were also the only ones on our block who didn't believe in Jesus Christ. We didn't believe in anything. Even though we didn't believe in Jesus Christ, we did celebrate Christmas. In December, my father strung white lights on the naked birch tree out front. We hung stockings by the fireplace and left a plate of cookies for Santa Claus, who came to our house just like he came to the Christians' houses. Some years, Santa gave me more presents than he gave the Christians. I wanted to know if the Cape Man was Jewish or Catholic or Protestant or Nothing, and my father said there is no Cape Man.

Mrs. Junot got a black eye, which she tried to hide behind a pair of dark glasses, but beneath the frames a blotch of purple and yellow showed.

My mother said it was peculiar the way Mr. Keyes doted on the twins—Andrea and Doria Keyes. He was the one who picked out their outfits, dressing them in frilly skirts and white socks with lace around the cuffs. He fixed their hair, plaiting it into French braids. Mrs. Keyes didn't wear makeup and was best friends with Mrs. Robison. Other neighbors whispered that the two women spent far too much time together.

I wished I could go to the Aqueduct. That was always the best part of summer, packing a cheese sandwich in a brown paper bag, filling a canteen with water, hiking between the trees, coming to rest by the stream, pretending to be lost in a forest far away from home, maybe never finding my way back, imagining what it would be like to sleep there and eat worms for survival. But I wasn't allowed to go to the Aqueduct alone, and no one else was allowed to go there because of the Cape Man.

Why couldn't the policemen catch the Cape Man if everyone knew that he lived in the Aqueduct? My father said it was because you can't catch your own shadow. I was bored. There was nothing fun to do.

A giant mosquito bit me, and my mother put calamine lotion on it. Calamine lotion looked like pink crud. My mother said don't scratch, but I couldn't help it and scratched until it bled.

Every Halloween there was talk of the lady who put razor blades in apples, but no one ever got one. We were supposed to throw away loose candy, but I didn't because I liked candy corns, especially the ones with the brown tips.

Pammy Barnett and I sat on the curb in front of my house playing jacks. Pammy cheated at jacks, making up rules as we went along. I wanted to smack Pammy Barnett but didn't because if you fought with Pammy, her mother would come and scream at you, and my mother wouldn't scream back at her. My mother said I had to fight my own battles, which I didn't think was fair because Mrs. Barnett was a grown-up, and I wasn't. Across the street, the Keyes twins sat side by side as if they were on display at a circus sideshow. They wore identical yellow pinafores and yellow ribbons in their hair. I wondered if I closed my eyes and then opened them, would Andrea and Doria be gone—poof!—as if they were never really there?

Pammy was on sixies when a blue Dodge Dart, exactly like the one Pammy's father drove, came down the street. Pammy called time out and yelled, "Daddy!" and raced over to the car. But it wasn't her father driving. A teenage boy was driving, and he put on his brakes because if he didn't, he might've run over Pammy Barnett. Another teenage boy was in the passenger seat. Pammy was staring at him like she couldn't figure out that there was more than one blue Dodge Dart in the world, when the teenage boy opened the car door and said, "You want to come with us, little girl?" It was all kind of funny, the same way it was funny when once in Macy's I bit a strange man on the leg. I thought the man I was biting was my father, whom I was furious at for refusing to buy me Barbie's Dream House. Only Pammy didn't think the teenage boys were funny. She ran home crying that they had tried to kidnap her. Mrs. Barnett called the police and said it was possible that one of the boys who tried to kidnap Pammy was the Cape Man by night, like in *I Was a Teenage Werewolf*.

The police came to talk to me because I was an eyewitness to the maybe attempted kidnapping of Pammy Barnett by maybe the Cape Man. The police sat in our living room. One of them had a notebook and was writing down what I said, only I wasn't sure what to say because I didn't think the teenage boys really wanted to kidnap Pammy, but I didn't want to disappoint the policemen and everybody else who thought we had a clue to catching the Cape Man.

Hide-and-seek was a game for night, and I hid between our garage and the shrubs where Kevin Robison found me, even though he wasn't It. He pushed me up against the garage wall and touched me down there. This was something he would do many times over many years, find me alone and cop a feel.

I hated where we lived and asked my mother if we could please move away. My mother said, "There is no Cape Man," but the Cape Man wasn't the reason why I wanted to move away. After school started, we heard the Cape Man was caught, although there wasn't any word of it in the newspaper. My mother said they had probably come across some poor, unsuspecting hobo sleeping in the woods and chased him off.

Virginia Brady planned to become a nun. Her mother always said Virginia's going to enter the convent, but she got pregnant instead. My mother said the poor kid probably didn't even know what she was doing.

Before bedtime, I sat at the kitchen table staring out into our backyard, which I could do then because that was before my parents added on a sunroom.

Mrs. Robison told my mother that even after twelve years of marriage and four children, not including the stillborn one, Mr. Robison had never seen her naked.

What was all the fuss about naked?

Once, the Martians were supposed to land, but they didn't. Another time, the world was supposed to come to an end, but that didn't happen either.

On some other night, another summer a few years later, under a hazy moon I sat on my swing in the backyard. Having grown too tall for it, my feet scuffed the ground. A cricket chirped, and the grass was freshly mowed, and across the lawn walked an armadillo. I watched it make its way along the path into the Robisons' yard, where it disappeared from view. As if it were the Pied Piper, I longed to follow it, to go somewhere away from here, but instead I went inside and told my parents I'd seen an armadillo in the yard. They laughed, and when they stopped laughing, my father said it was probably a cat or a skunk. "I wouldn't try to pet that armadillo if I were you," he said. My mother added, "You better keep that imagination of yours in check, young lady." My parents said there were no armadillos in Westchester. Admittedly, it was a creature that didn't belong there, but I'd seen it still.

It would be another five years before I finally snitched on Kevin Robison. I told his sister Kathleen, "Your brother is always grabbing me, touching me." Kathleen told her mother, and Mrs. Robison, livid and red in the face from rage, came to our house and called me a dirty-minded, lying little slut. My mother told me to forget about it, that Mrs. Robison had problems, but I didn't forget about it.

Perhaps I was a bit sleepy on such a hot summer night and so near to my bedtime, but I did see him from out the kitchen window. First, a glimmer of silver in the dark like a shooting star, and then I saw, not so much as his cape, but the movement of it, swirling around him as he came closer to me. I ran to the den where my parents were watching a man roller-skate on a barrel on *Ed Sullivan*, and I said I saw him! He's out there! The Cape Man!

But my father said, no, you didn't, and my mother said, that's it, off to bed with you, and I said, really he's there. I saw him. I saw his silver hands. I saw his cape.

My parents didn't even get up to look. "Bed." My mother pointed off in the direction of my room.

I did not get into bed but went to my window, which faced not the backyard but out front. I did not see the Cape Man again. Instead, I saw the houses on my block, quiet and neat and all looking pretty much the same from the outside, and I remembered what my father had said, that you can't catch shadows. Not even when they're at your window pressing silver hands against the glass.

rural delivery

NOVEMBER 19, 1992
One Week Before Thanksgiving

I'm optimistic, but not entirely. Bill Clinton says he's a new Democrat. I liked the old Democrats just fine. Still, the twelve-year reign of the Republicans is over, and to my mind, that is reason enough to be thankful.

Another reason to be thankful is this day, the sun is shining, the air is crisp. Rudy, Lorraine's child, is spending the weekend with her family in Farmville, so Lorraine and I can journey across the border into North Carolina, to the Blue Ridge Mountains.

Chase City, where Lorraine lives, is flat. It's tobacco country. Before now, at the close of each of my visits, she'd promise, "Next time. Next time you come, we'll go to the mountains."

I like mountains. The way some people find the beach to be idyllic, I seek my solace in tall, craggy peaks, in the dip of a valley or a hollow, in the dark pine trees shrouding the landscape. A person can lie low in the mountains, whereas at the beach there's no place to hide. At the beach, you're a sitting duck. New York City, my home, is relatively level ground, but the skyline—building blocks of refuge—is not unlike a mountain range beckoning you to look up.

Lorraine's got a map spread out on her kitchen table. "Here." She points. "This is where we'll go. Pilot's Mountain. Mount Airy."

Although I couldn't ever have been there, Mount Airy has a ring of the familiar, like I know someone from there, which I don't.

"Of course it sounds familiar," Lorraine says. "Mount Airy is Mayberry. And Pilot's Mountain is Mount Pilot. From *The Andy Griffith Show*. Everybody knows Mayberry. It's famous. Like Pamplona."

Mayberry. I'm going to Mayberry. As a child, I had extensive and elaborate fantasies about living in Mayberry, of sitting on my front porch, of knowing everyone in town by name. I'd begged my mother please, please can't we move to Mayberry, but my mother said, "That's television. There's no such place." Evidently, my mother was mistaken.

Despite that Mount Airy is only a few hours' drive from Chase City, Lorraine has never been there before either. Except to visit kinfolk, family, Southerners tend to stay put. They settle into that red soil like it's quicksand. Lorraine has been to the Blue Ridge Mountains only to go to Galax, where her father's family is from. So much does Lorraine now stay in one place that, although she lives in a big house, she rarely ventures from the living room. She sits, eats, sleeps, reads, watches television, all in one chair in front of a wood-burning stove. "You don't need this big house," I tell her often. "All you really want is a studio apartment."

The funny thing is that when Lorraine lived in New York, she was the most mobile person I knew. In eight years, she lived in six different apartments. Moving as if there were a fire underfoot, she fled from Manhattan to Brooklyn to Queens and back to Manhattan. Lorraine worked as a travel agent only because she got free airfare. She went to the Mideast, to Europe, to South America, the way she now goes to the Red Lion Supermarket and Judy's Beauty Salon. To meet Lorraine in Chase City, you'd never guess that she'd been practically everywhere, that she'd taken the most circuitous road home.

LATER THE SAME DAY
Somewhere Near the Border

The road is desolate. The pine trees grow tall and thick and allow only splinters of sunlight to break through the canopy. It's been a while since we passed another car. "Why," Lorraine asks, "is it always creepy near a border? It doesn't matter which border. It's all hainted territory."

I light a cigarette and explain, "It's because everyone, except for a few lunatics, scrambles clear of demarcations, for fear of winding up on the wrong side." Lorraine knows this perfectly well because of Peter, her ex and one true love. After World War II, he wound up in what became Czechoslovakia. Being outside their own line impelled his mother to put him, a toddler then, into a bathtub, and as if it were a wagon, she dragged the tub with her child in it across the Sudetenland, refusing to stop until she reached Hanau, a town outside Frankfurt. She'd calculated Hanau to be far from any border.

We pass more trees and then a small clearing. A wooden house with a sagging front porch has a sign out front, a sign like a FOR SALE sign, only this sign is for a MONSTER MUSEUM AND GIFT SHOP.

By the time Lorraine pulls off to the side of the road, we've passed the place. She twists in her seat to look back and asks, "Do we dare?"

"I think we have to," I say. "We'll regret it if we don't."

We follow the arrows for the MONSTER MUSEUM AND GIFT SHOP around to the back of the house. The screen door opens into the gift shop. On a chair by the register a young man sits reading a comic book. His skin is as white as rubber. Blue veins traverse his face and hands like a road map. We keep our distance from him while we poke around the shop, checking the price tags on Frankenstein masks, plastic fangs, New Age crystals, and witch ointments.

Lorraine wants to buy a bottle of potion labeled *Money*. As of late, Lorraine has taken to believing that a large infu-

sion of cash would solve her problems; that if she were suddenly to come into a bundle of money, she would pick up the
pieces of her life and arrange them so they fit. No matter how
past experience tells Lorraine that no one thing—not one
house, not one Democrat, not one plane ticket, not one pile
of cash—can straighten out the whole mess, she continues to
pray for a windfall. If Lorraine ever came across a magic lamp
or a monkey's paw, she'd be in big trouble.

I choose a potion that offers *Success*. There was a time, not
all that long ago, when Lorraine and I would not have so
much as glanced at *Money* and *Success*. We would've beelined
for the *Love* lotion. We would've doused ourselves in *Passion*
oil, bathed in the goop called *Romance*. But we rarely talk
of such things anymore. Not since Lorraine got a letter,
unsigned, telling her that Peter had cancer. Lorraine suspected that the note came from Peter's mother because
mothers can never resist women who are truly in love with
their sons.

Lorraine supposes that, by this point, Peter is either dead
or peeing into a bag. Either way, it's the end. Actually the end
came before that, when Peter went home to Frankfurt and
married the cross-eyed girl he'd been living with for seventeen years. As for me, I'm older and I know some things now.
I know that you can't have everything.

We take our vials of *Money* and *Success* to the cash register, where we see a flyer advertising tarot card readings for
one dollar. I ask the pasty-skinned guy where we can get our
cards read, and he beckons us to follow him as he disappears
behind a curtain.

Lorraine looks at me as if to ask, *Are we're going to get out of here alive?* Lorraine is always telling me stories about Southern sickos. Crazies who tie women to trees and chainsaw off their arms and legs. That kind of thing.

Behind the curtain is a small room, the foyer to the Monster Museum. Tattered posters of Boris Karloff and Lon Chaney are tacked to the walls. I don't think the museum would be worth the two bucks admission.

Lorraine and I sit in a pair of frayed armchairs as if we were here for a visit. The pasty-skinned guy sets up a card table, takes a seat next to me, and shuffles a deck of cards. I can't look at his face. It's too white and too creepy. My eyes roam and come to rest at the bulge in his pants.

He lays out eleven cards and studies them. "You're going to profit from an immoral act," he tells me.

There is money in Lorraine's future and a series of no-good men in her past. Also, he sees change in her life. Possibly a new job, a better-paying job than she's got. That is unlikely. Lorraine teaches high school English, which is as fine a job as there is to be had in Chase City.

When we get outside, Lorraine says, "He was good with those cards, don't you think?"

I agree, and I don't mention that our purchases of *Money* and *Success* oils surely tipped him off. But I do add, "He had a boner a half mile high."

"How do you know that?" Lorraine asks.

"I saw." I get into the car and buckle my seat belt.

Lorraine slides into the driver's seat. "What do you mean *you saw*? Why were looking at that spooky guy's wang?"

"I couldn't look at his face. It gave me the chills."

"So you look at his dick?"

"Where else do you look?" I ask, and Lorraine wants to know, "So how big was it? Was it a full-blown hard-on? Or just a little bit starched?"

"Big. Big and stiff and pushing up out of his pants like a mountain rising up from a valley."

MOUNT AIRY/MAYBERRY
An Altered State

It doesn't say Floyd's, but this *is* Floyd's Barber Shop. There's a pole out front and the sign TWO CHAIRS. NO WAITING. Lorraine and I venture inside, and sure enough, there's Floyd. He's older than when I last saw him twenty-something years ago cutting Andy's hair in black and white. But that's Floyd. I'd know him anywhere.

He leaves his customer with one sideburn longer than the other to chat with Lorraine and me about the weather. Just as he did when I watched him on TV, Floyd rambles, which gets on my nerves. Floyd was always my least favorite citizen of Mayberry. "We have to be going now," I tell him.

"Well, you all come back tomorrow," Floyd says, "so I can take your picture."

We walk along Main Street, and Lorraine says, "I'm confused. Was that an actor playing Floyd the barber? Or is he a barber they put on TV?"

"Beats me," I say, but I do expect to see Barney and

Thelma Lou strolling hand in hand along Main Street, and Andy and Opie—fishing poles over their shoulders— heading out to the lake. I also think that if I were to call my mother right now, Donna Reed would answer the phone, and my father would say to her, "Give my love to Kitten." I'd have a brother named Beaver, and the worst thing that could happen to me is that I'd get handcuffed to Lucy.

We don't look when we cross the street—there are no messy accidents in Mayberry—to go to the drugstore, where we sit at the luncheonette counter. I assume the ice cream here is homemade, but I ask for scrambled eggs and toast.

Lorraine leans in to tell me that in the South you don't eat breakfast for supper the way you do in New York. However, the woman at the griddle is happy to oblige me, and in that case, Lorraine will have eggs and toast and sausages, as well.

While we wait for our food, the mayor comes in for pie and coffee. Florid-faced and fat, he's stuffed into a light-weight suit. He wears white shoes even though it's well after Labor Day, and he takes the seat next to Otis, the town drunk. Sporting a five-o'clock shadow and wearing last week's clothes, Otis nurses a hangover and grins like a jack-o'-lantern at Lorraine. The mayor eyeballs me and winks.

That mayor is as greasy as the eggs slithering around on my plate. "You see," Lorraine says to me, "the ones with money always go for you. He's got money, that one. I can tell. And look who goes for me. The good-for-nothing drunk. Isn't that always the way?"

I eat my toast and drink my coffee while Lorraine tries to

cozy up to the mayor. "Could you recommend a place for us to stay the night?" Her tone is almost suggestive.

He directs us to a motel that is on the outskirts of town and where he probably gets a kickback. I know a sleazeball when I see one.

"Yeah," Lorraine says, "but a sleazeball with money."

I shake my head at her, and Lorraine says, "Come on, admit it. Some money would help."

"Help with what?" I ask, but Lorraine can't answer that. "Everything," she says.

THE NEXT DAY IT DAWNS ON ME
You Can't Live on Television
Even If You've Got Cable

Episodes of *The Andy Griffith Show* come flooding back to me: Aunt Bee gets canning jars for her birthday, Otis rides a donkey, Andy captures escaped convicts, Opie shoots a bird—even though I haven't seen the show for years and years. Lorraine, on the other hand, has cable and gets Mayberry in reruns. For her, this is more immediate and less like a dream.

The menu at Snappy Lunch, where Andy and Barney ate nearly every episode, offers bologna sandwiches and hamburgers (breaded or all-meat), but what Snappy Lunch is really famous for is their pork sandwich. I don't eat pork, but Lorraine does. The chop is breaded, deep-fried, and smothered in lard-laden onions between two slices of white bread.

Lorraine considers this a meal consisting of the four major food groups.

Lorraine, an otherwise intelligent and worldly woman, is ignorant when it comes to nutrition. Ten years before, despite how she detested Ronald Reagan—and she did take his triumphs poorly and to heart—she didn't understand the ketchup-as-vegetable fuss. "It *is* tomatoes," Lorraine had said.

I have seen Rudy drink soy sauce from the bottle and eat Reese's Peanut Butter Cups for dinner. Lorraine encouraged her child to eat broccoli only to smite George Bush.

"This is good." Lorraine wipes grease from her lips with a paper napkin. "You sure you won't have one?"

"Positive." I nibble at my grilled cheese sandwich.

Reflecting on her own situation now as a single mother, her ex-husband out of work and drunk and living in some broken-down trailer in the woods, Lorraine says, "Andy was a single parent. And look how fine that Opie turned out. Grows up to be a big movie director."

"That's true," I say. "Ron Howard is a son to be proud of."

We keep our promise to return to Floyd's. He takes three pictures of us with his Polaroid camera. One for Lorraine, one for me, and one goes up on the barbershop wall. Then Floyd tells us to wait. "I got gifts too for you pretty ladies." He shuffles to the back of the shop to get each of us a picture postcard of Wally's Service Station, where Goober and Gomer worked until Gomer joined the Marines and got a TV show of his own. That was before everyone knew Gomer was gay. A gay marine wouldn't have gotten his own sitcom back then.

Floyd also gives us pictures of Frances Bavier's house on

Main Street. She was the one who played Aunt Bee. After being Aunt Bee for so long, she must've gotten confused and moved from Hollywood to Mayberry as if to stay at home.

Back out on the street, it is Lorraine who mentions that all the people in Mayberry are white. "You notice that? I never saw a Southern town that didn't have some black folk. But look around," she says. "What do you see?"

I look up and down Main Street. I see a town where no one is black or Hispanic or Korean or Jewish or Greek. I see a town so isolated that no one even reads a newspaper. There is no president of the United States—Democrat or Republican—in Mayberry. Here the only elected officials are the mayor and the sheriff, who doesn't even carry a gun. This is a town where, if you've got cable, the people come to life for half-hour segments to go fishing, to go courting, to bake a pie. No one's living in poverty. There's no graffiti on the buildings. There are no serial killers here. No senseless slaughter. The worst thing that could happen in Mayberry is you get handcuffed by mistake to Barney.

And I know now that my mother was right: Mayberry is not a real place. At least not for me.

BACK TO CHASE CITY
It Was a Southerner Who Said
You Can't Go Home Again

It seems to be close to midnight when we get back to Lorraine's house, but in fact it's just after six. It's not that it gets darker earlier here, but the dark is deeper. There are no streetlights, no neon signs to soften the night. Only the occasional blue glow from a television set cuts into the pitch.

In our coats, we sit on the front porch. It's a bit nippy out, but the sky is clear and the stars look like silver glitter.

"You hungry?" Lorraine asks. "I got a bucket of Hardee's chicken in the fridge. I can pop it in the microwave."

Wordlessly, as if we'd planned it—but we didn't—we carry her kitchen table out to the porch. Lorraine takes her good china from the highboy. I get the crystal candlesticks and two lavender tapers.

On this November night, we eat Hardee's fried chicken and drink Coca-Cola by candlelight under the sky, under the stars, under the gaze of the neighbors peering out from between the slats of venetian blinds. A car drives up Sycamore Street and then circles the block twice, slowing down in front of Lorraine's house as if we were a tourist attraction or an accident on the highway. Soon more cars come, and I tell Lorraine, "This happens in Long Island during the Christmas season when some family goes overboard with the decorations."

"Just ignore them," Lorraine instructs. "Bunch of rubes never saw anyone dine alfresco before."

Later, over coffee, when all the gawkers have given up and gone home, when everything is so still you can feel your pulse beating, I hear the sorrowful low of a cow. And then another. And another, until the whole herd is mooing. I sit and listen, and then Lorraine says, "Do you hear cows?"

"Yeah," I say.

"There's something wrong," she tells me. "No one around here keeps cows." Lorraine wants to find out which of her neighbors snuck a herd of cows by her, and I just want to see them.

Away from the porch light, Lorraine is but a presence in the dark, a shadow guiding me. We walk, following the sound of the plaintive lows, but because it grows neither louder nor softer, I wonder, "Are we walking in circles?"

"No," Lorraine assures me, but she wants reassurance too. "You do hear them, don't you? You do hear cows?"

"Yes, I hear them. And you hear them. But why are we the only ones out here looking for them? We have dinner on the porch and half the town turns out to gawk, but now we're the only ones curious."

"Okay," Lorraine says. "Let's assume there are no cows. So what then are we hearing?"

But there are cows. There must be cows. We just haven't found them. Still, I tease Lorraine and say, "Flying saucers always land in places like this."

Lorraine doesn't buy that explanation. "These are ghosts. Hainted spirits. That's what's calling us. Ghosts. Ghosts think they're going to fool me by making noises like cows."

"Why would ghosts pretend to be cows?" I ask, and Lorraine says, "To keep me here, to keep me walking in circles looking for them."

I worry that with all landmarks veiled in the night, we won't find our way back to Lorraine's house, that we will wander lost and confused. But Lorraine's got the instincts of a homing pigeon, and we are soon standing at the path leading to her porch.

The candle flames dance to stay alive. The Royal Dalton cups and saucers are waiting for us to sit down and finish our coffee as if we'd never been lured away by a kind of siren's song. But we stay put at the foot of the path, looking on as if the porch, the table, the candles, and the cups were a photograph, eerie and timeless. I half expect Minna and Lucie—the two long-dead crazy sisters who first owned Lorraine's house—to come to the door, to wave us in to join them, when Lorraine says, "It was a mistake to come back."

I assume Lorraine means we should still be searching for the cows, until she walks the path to the porch, climbs the three steps. "It's time I left here for good," Lorraine says, and she blows out the candles.